COZY CASITA CHRISTMAS

TE SHERIDAN

Cozy Casita Christmas

by

TE Sheridan

Contemporary Romance Novella

Published by TE Sheridan

Edited by A. Marie

Cover by Redbird Design

Copyright © 2020

ISBN#: 978-1-951637-19-4

CHAPTER 1

SAVI

The topless chick on the patio was unexpected.

Not that he was complaining.

Savion Merchant wandered across the living room, his loafers making a soft thud on the white marble tiled floor and stood at the glass door. Definitely topless. He could step outside to get a better look, but she would most likely hear the door and come unglued about him being on the patio, and all hell would break loose.

Because he was supposed to be alone here this week.

He just needed a damned breather, somewhere to hide out for the holidays, put his feet up, and forget some stuff. The woman shifted slightly on the lounge chair. Savi tugged at the collar of his button-down shirt when she bent her knee, giving him a nice view of what appeared to be a perfectly lean inner thigh. If she hadn't moved just now, he might have thought she was sleeping. She appeared utterly relaxed, her nipples soft and pink. Savi eyed his hands for a moment and then looked back at the woman's breasts.

How long had it been since he'd touched a woman?

Hell, for that matter, how long had it been since he'd jacked off in the shower and thought of a woman? Any woman. Way too damned long. Which is one of the reasons why he was in Phoenix for the holiday. Some much needed Savion time.

And while Lane Taylor was a good friend, setting him up with a place to stay for however long he wanted to be here over Christmas, Savi doubted his generosity extended to providing strippers or female companions. And even if Lane were so inclined, Savi doubted Lane's wife would be in favor.

Which meant the chick on the patio was not expecting him. And she might come after him and gouge his eyes out or chop his dick off if she happened to open her eyes and catch him watching her sunbathe.

Still, he propped his shoulder on the doorframe, hungry eyes glued to the beautiful bare breasts on display. Blair was beautiful; even after all these years, she was still beautiful. Just not his to look at or love anymore. The chick on the patio wore a tiny bikini bottom; from the angle with her knee bent and the bottom of a smooth ass cheek bared to him, Savi couldn't be sure it wasn't a thong.

He'd love to know.

For a moment, he imagined kneeling there on the edge of her chair and leaning over to flick his tongue in her belly button and scrape his teeth over the scrap of black between her legs. The ring of his cell phone snapped him out of his thoughts—what the hell was wrong with him? He did not entertain midday sexual fantasies, and he did not gape at naked women unless they were on TV or in the spread of glossy magazine pages. And even then, Savion Merchant didn't overindulge.

He started to pull his phone from the pocket of his trousers, but the woman on the patio apparently heard his ringtone, also. He didn't do cute rings, didn't do funny stuff. The sound that had jarred him from his fantasies and her from her sunbathing was the default ring on his smart phone. Savi glanced at the screen, only partly relieved to see it was Lane calling. Lane could clear this up, tell him why there was a topless woman sunbathing on the patio that he had been told would be exclusively his for the next seven days, if he so desired.

But the woman on the other side of the glass door was scrambling to cover herself now, eyes on Savi, as if she feared he had just broken into the Taylor's house to pillage the place and rape her. Probably best to deal with her first and then return Lane's call.

Decision made, he slipped the phone back in his pocket and slid the door open. December in Phoenix was a world away from December in Milwaukee. Still, Savi felt a slight breeze as he stepped outside. If this chick had been in the water at all, she had to be cold. Obviously, she hadn't. Her hair was dry. And before now, before she yanked the blue and white striped beach towel up to cover herself, her nipples certainly weren't erect, as if she had been lying wet with a breeze teasing her bare skin.

"Who are you? And what the fuck are you doing here?"

Her savage growl stopped Savi in his tracks just a few

steps outside the door. The woman wrapped the towel tightly around her body and held it firmly in her fist between her breasts. Her thick honeyed voice did things to him, the same kind of things her nipples had a few minutes ago. The same kind of things her long, lean legs were still doing.

"I'm callin' the cops." She turned away from him to march back toward the pool. Savi saw her snatch a cell phone from the small, white resin table by her chair.

"Don't call the police!"

Rather than assure her he was harmless, Savi's yelp seemed to send her into more of a panic. The woman turned to face him as she scrambled backwards over her chair. She wobbled on her feet for a second, but Savi only held his breath and waited for her to steady herself. If he rushed to her side to help her, she would probably throat punch him and shove him into the pool.

"I'm Lane's friend." He held his hands up in a peace gesture. "Savion Merchant. I'm staying here for a few days."

"Lane's friend?" she repeated. Her chest rose and fell on her quick, sharp breaths; the hand holding the towel between her breasts still clutched it tightly.

"Yes. I'm in town for the holidays."

"Lane and his wife are out of town," she hedged. Savi flinched. The woman didn't trust him. And he had only himself to blame. The decent thing to do when he found her sunbathing topless would have been to turn around and walk away and call Lane. Or knock on the door to alert her to his presence. Instead, Savi had done the most reckless thing he could do, probably the most reckless thing he'd done since his college days.

"Lane and Toni are in Colorado." He nodded. "I know that. They're celebrating the holidays with their family. I know. Lane set me up to stay here for a few days. I can call him."

The woman tipped her head and searched his face for a moment as he took a few cautious steps closer to her.

"Well, maybe you should call him." She shrugged, but she stared at him with a smug look on her face. "Because Toni told me I could stay here for the holidays, and that I would have the place to myself."

"Clearly," he mumbled.

"Excuse me?"

"Do you do that a lot?" The question tumbled out of his mouth before he could snap it shut.

"Do what? A lot?" She shook her head.

"Sunbathe nude?"

Savi was flustered now. Damn the woman for staring at him with that stupid little cocky grin on her face. He waved his hand at her body now covered with the towel.

"I wasn't nude," she argued.

"Close enough." He looked away. Ridiculous. He was a doctor, for God's sake. And he was blushing while referring to the fact that less than five minutes ago, he had been staring at this woman's tits.

Breasts.

Doctor of medicine, he reminded himself. A grown, mature man who practiced medicine and did not refer to a woman's body parts in derogatory terms. Was the word *tits* derogatory, though? Not medically correct, maybe not politically correct, but was it wrong to think of them that way? Blair had hated the word, but did all women?

"I was topless," the woman huffed, still irritated with him. "Not nude."

"Okay, but do you do that often?"

"Really?"

"You could burn," he reminded her. "And repeated exposure to the sun can cause skin cancer."

"You wear a top when you're in a pool?" she asked pointedly.

"Well, no. But—"

"Right." She nodded. "You're gonna need to call Lane. And find a different place to stay."

"I'm gonna have to find a different place?" Savi lifted his hand and scrubbed his fingers through his hair. "Why should I be the one to leave?"

This wasn't like him, either. Arguing. Never mind that the woman was as good as naked under the towel. Savion Merchant was even-tempered, mild-mannered, and an all-around good guy. Most people seemed to like that about him. His wife? Nope. Blair had most definitely thrown that at him as yet another shortcoming when she left him.

Which was a few years ago, true, and no, Savi didn't live in the past. It hurt when she left, but he was doing okay. He even dated after the divorce. Slept with enough women that his needs were filled, but never enough to tarnish his good-guy reputation at the clinic. Even after he stopped dating, he still found sex when he needed it. Kept his rep in check.

And then whammie. Blair got engaged. He and Blair's kids lived with Blair. They would live with Blair and Micah after the wedding. That burned his ass. Not Blair.

He had loved her, but never blindly. They'd had their problems from the get-go, and they'd had some good times, and when she left, Savi drank a little too much and took up boxing and broke a toe when he kicked a punching bag. But he got over Blair.

Just not his kids. Leaving. Living with her. With her and the new husband when they returned from their honeymoon holiday a week into the new year.

"Toni and I worked out these details before Thanksgiving," the woman announced.

Well, maybe she had him beat there. Lane had offered the casita to Savi the first week of December when Lane was in Milwaukee on business. They'd had dinner and drinks, and after too many drinks, Savi spilled the details about Blair and Micah getting married over Christmas. About the four of them—the happy couple and Savi's kids —going to the mountains in upstate New York to celebrate Christmas with Blair's family. The kids staying with her parents while she and Micah flew to Belize for a honeymoon for sand, surf, and sex.

"I'm not leaving."

"When did Lane say you could stay?"

"The first week of December," Savi answered, but he shrugged and shook his head. "But I'm not leaving."

He waited, assuming she would rail on him again. Threaten to call the cops. Call Toni. Chase him out the front.

"You gonna sic Chainsaw on me?" he asked after a few moments. He realized suddenly that there was music playing from Lane's high-tech surround sound speakers in the backyard. Savi took a moment to appreciate the rest of the view out here: the long rectangular pool with sparkling, perfectly blue water, the tennis and basketball court, and the firepit and gazebo. The property was immaculate, but then Lane and Toni had always been that way, so none of it should come as a surprise to Savi now. None of it except the woman who was now watching him with a smirk on her face.

"What?"

"Chainsaw's a teddy bear." She rolled her eyes. True. The German Shepherd put the fear of God in a lot of people, but the dog was a lover, not a fighter. "And besides, Toni took him to the doggy hotel."

"Nope." Savi squeezed his eyes closed. "They got someone new to watch him. A place that only takes two or three dogs in at a time."

"Right."

Savi was shocked that the woman agreed with something he said.

"Look."

He did. She still had the towel knotted in a fist between her breasts. Savi still wanted to see a little more, but he was quick to avert his gaze up to meet her eyes.

"It's a big house." She sighed.

"Technically, I'm in the casita," he mumbled.

"Okay. Well, you have the casita. I'm in the guest suite in the house."

"You're calling a truce?"

"Only because I can lock you out of the main part of the house."

"Because I look so dangerous, right?" He arched his brows at her. The woman made no secret of checking him out. Sweat rolled down the middle of his back, and his dick stretched to greet her when her eyes roamed low, below his belt.

"You were staring at my tits." She delivered her reminder calmly, a little flick of her eyebrow giving away that she was still irritated.

"Admiring the view."

"Please tell me that line hasn't worked for you before."

Savi hadn't used a line since before he and Blair were married. And the last one he had used—whatever it was— had been used on Blair, and the thought that thousands of miles away just now Aszia and Drew were in a mountain chalet with Blair and Micah, eating cookies and talking about the wedding, made his head pound.

"I can honestly say I've never come upon a topless woman sunbathing and been able to use the line at all."

"Yeah?" She grinned. "Do you get out much? You need another look?"

She was dicking with him, but the smile on her face was friendly enough.

"Because if not, I think I'm going to go in and shower."

He nodded as the woman slipped by him, close enough that he could smell the coconut and lime on her skin.

"Do you have a name?" he asked. "Or should I just call you Titsy?"

Again, he was stunned by what he said, by the fact that he actually let the words fly. He turned to watch her as she neared the door he had come through to be outside. She looked at him over her shoulder and laughed softly.

"That's pretty good," she chuckled. "My last boyfriend offered to buy me a boob job. Said I didn't have enough for his liking."

"Must have been pretty damned picky," Savi said quietly.

"I'm Mia Griffey." She pulled the door back and stepped inside, leaving Savi alone with Tina Turner singing "What's Love Got To Do With It."

CHAPTER 2

Mia

She hurried through her shower, her stomach a quivering little mess of nerves. There was a guy on the property. A stranger. Just because he knew Toni and Lane didn't mean he was a good guy. He had stood in the house and stared at her boobs for who knows how long? How long would he have stayed there if his phone hadn't rung and given him away?

Then again, he seemed okay when she confronted him. He had kept his distance from her. And judging from what he said about Toni and Lane, even about Chainsaw, he did know them.

Still, the knowledge that she wasn't alone—never mind that she *could* lock him completely out of the main house and *had* locked him out of the guest suite—made her speed her way through the shower. She hadn't been outside that long; her flight got in late last night, and she had stayed up late watching 80s movies, which she had found stacked in the closet in her bedroom. She slept late this morning, had coffee and an egg while she checked her email, and had only been out in the sun less than an hour when Lane's friend set up shop to watch her.

Mia slapped some coconut body butter over her arms and legs. Careful to rub it in everywhere, she eyed her reflection in the oversized, oval mirror over the white marble vanity. Her belly and her breasts were no pinker than any other area of skin she had left exposed earlier, though her breasts—nipples especially—were sensitive to her touch. Had nothing to do with the sun and sadly, everything to do with Lane's sexy friend.

He was buttoned up, sure, but he had a beautiful face, and even when she wanted to be outraged at him earlier, he had given her a grin that had been like flipping a switch to turn on her sex-starved body. His button-down shirt and expensive trousers fit as if they had been tailor-made for him. Mia couldn't deny that she would have liked a closer look at him. Maybe, if they shared the patio and pool spaces, she would get to see a little more of that body. Enough to fuel some sexy fantasies, maybe. Not that she would admit that to Toni or Lane.

After blowing her blond hair dry, she eyed herself in the mirror once more and decided to forego any makeup. She was here on vacation, after all, and in the event that she did see Savion again, she wasn't here to impress him anyway. She stepped into the adjoining bedroom naked and eyed her closed and locked bedroom door. When she had come inside, she automatically checked her phone.

Three missed calls from Toni. And an SOS text. About she and Lane miscommunicating. And Lane's friend Savi coming to stay in the casita, just as an FYI. Mia texted back before she showered. Told her the FYI came a little late, and that Savi had caught her outback topless. The answering text was a string of about seven laughing and crying emojis and then another five flames.

Mia dressed in plain black cotton panties, capri sweatpants, and a loose-fitting white T-shirt that said *let it snow*. On her way out the door, she hesitated, wondering if she should put a bra on, but she decided it against it. She was on vacation. Savion was in the casita, which meant she shouldn't have to see him. And she planned to find something for dinner and then curl up outside again with a book and a glass of wine.

The house was silent when she returned to the kitchen. Done in shades of white, gold and gray and accentuated with splashes of orange, the décor in the Taylor house looked like something out of a magazine. Mia padded barefoot to the refrigerator and snatched the Chardonnay she'd chilled earlier.

Her parents were in Greece for the holiday. They celebrated their thirty-fifth wedding anniversary the week before Thanksgiving, so this was their trip. Mia and her sister and brother loved that they were finally taking time for themselves, even if it was over the holidays. Mia's brother was celebrating Christmas in Texas with his girlfriend's family, and her sister and her family were back in Iowa with her brother-in-law's family. Of course, they had invited Mia to join them, but Mia politely refused the invite. She loved her brother-in-law but thought her sister was a saint to have married into that family. Christmas here in Phoenix would be perfect. She had plenty of reading material with her. Plenty of wine. Sunshine. She never left home without her laptop, so she could work from anywhere, and she had a few other friends in the Phoenix area that she planned to visit.

She and her family planned to celebrate Christmas in January when everyone was back at home.

Still, a little something Christmasy might be nice. Lane and Toni's tree in the far corner of the room beckoned. She had noticed it last night, of course, but she hadn't turned the lights on. Maybe now she would. The tree lights and a little bit of music with her dinner. Why not?

Mia flipped the light switch by the glass door and sighed with contentment when the corner lit up with twinkling white lights. She took a second to admire some of the ornaments, particularly the ones she knew Toni's girls had made through the years. Toni and Lane got married and had kids young, hence their head start on Mia. Married for nine years and their girls were already eight and six. Mia graduated from college with Toni, but she was still single, still hoping to have the husband and kids and dream house one day.

She stepped away from the tree and backed into the kitchen, eyes loving the glow of the lights. Ready for more cheer, Mia accessed a music app on her phone and turned on a playlist of holiday music.

Perfect.

All of the magic of Christmasy things, minus the below zero temperatures and the dreaded ice and snow of home.

Eyes on the wine bottle as she tugged the cork from it, she jumped and spun around when she heard the door between the casita and the main house open.

"Got a second?" Savion peeked his head in. She had left the door unlocked, because it sort of seemed…rude…to lock him out of the house. But she would have to remember that when she went to bed. She didn't know this guy. Didn't know how he knew Lane and Toni. Didn't know if he walked in his sleep and would end up in the main house. If he was always a perv who liked to watch women when they weren't aware that he was there.

"Sure." She finally pulled the cork free and set it on the counter. Propping one foot on top of the other, she twisted at the counter to look at him as he stepped inside.

"I'm heading to the grocery store," he announced. "Just wondered if you need anything."

Okay, so that was nice.

And he had changed clothes. His loose-fit black shorts hung off his hips and called attention to his hard, muscular-looking thighs and calves. Mia guessed he spent some time on a bike. The gray T-shirt loved his wide shoulders and chest, and he had traded his black loafers for worn athletic flip-flops.

She had been right.

Sexy as fuck.

Definitely gonna lock the door tonight. Maybe she should ask Toni if Savi could lock his door from his side.

"I think I'm good." She was a little bit sad to admit that. It would be nice to have a list of things she needed so she had an excuse for seeing him again.

"You know where the closest store is?"

"There's one about three miles up the main road," she answered. "Basic grocery store with some limited health food aisles."

"Do I look like a health food guy?"

She looked up at the note of amusement in his voice. Hell yes, he did. He looked like whole grains, egg whites, and protein shakes. A fifteen-mile bike ride and bench pressing his body weight kind of guy.

Maybe like a guy who could go all night long.

Mia cleared her throat and looked back at the wine bottle.

"Well, no," she lied, "but since you were concerned about me getting sun burnt or skin cancer." She shrugged, poured her wine, and looked up at him innocently.

His eyes were on her breasts. The T-shirt was loose enough, but at the moment, it was pulled tight, her fully erect nipples on display. A little bit embarrassed, she considered pretending to shiver.

Why bother? The guy had seen her completely topless not too long ago.

Instead, she kept her eyes on him and waited for him to look up.

"Do you have something against wearing clothing over your breasts?"

"I have a shirt on." She rolled her eyes. "And did you seriously say breasts? What are you? Like eighty?"

"You have a shirt on that appears to be made solely for the purpose of outlining your nipples." He arched an eyebrow. "The same nipples that are not hidden behind a bra."

"You're saying you want me to put a bra on?"

"Not saying that at all." He shook his head.

"'kay." Mia huffed and flashed him a smile. "I mean, you've already seen everything there is to see, right? I'm on vacation. I'd rather not put a bra on right now."

"Right." He nodded.

Mia sipped her wine and watched a little tidal wave of heat inch up his neck and into his cheeks.

"Do you want some?" she asked him.

"I'm sorry?"

"Wine." She cleared her throat. "Would you like a glass of wine?"

"Yes." He laughed, and the sound was genuine and happy. "That sounds great."

She stepped around him, close enough to feel his body heat, and grabbed a second glass from the cabinet.

"How do you know Lane?" she asked as she poured. She kept her eyes on the wine, but from the corner of her eye, she saw him set his keys and phone on the counter.

"Went to college with him."

"Yeah? In Milwaukee?"

"Yep."

"And where do you live now?" Mia nudged the glass closer to him, but she pulled her hand away before he reached for it.

"Milwaukee," he answered with a small grin. "You?"

"Iowa." She reached for her phone, intending to turn the music off, but Savi stopped her with the slightest press of his fingers on the back of her hand.

"Let it play," he suggested.

Mia studied his face for a moment and finally nodded. An instrumental version of "Sleigh Ride" started, making her feel festive. Even if she had just been lounging outside by the pool.

"Toni and I played ball together in school," she told him.

Savion stared at her for a moment. She was uncomfortable under his intense gaze, but she refused to squirm.

"You look like an outfielder."

"Excuse me?" She tipped her head. Heat surged up her neck to her face when he made a show of checking out her legs.

"Long legs. I'm guessing you played centerfield."

He was right. She played outfield, most often center-field, because she was fast and could cover a lot of ground. She had a shotgun arm, too, but he was still focused on her legs.

"So, you played ball?"

"Nope." He shook his head. "I was the nerdy math and science guy. Played a little trumpet. I could hold my own in a pickup game, but I wasn't into organized sports."

"A nerdy math and science guy," Mia repeated. She carried her glass to the living room and sank down on one end of the luxurious stone-colored sofa. The tree stood a few feet to her left; the open living and kitchen space spread out to her right. Savion sipped his wine, but he stayed put at the counter. "And you were friends with Lane?"

Savion laughed softly. "Right? We met freshman year in composition."

"Tell me something funny about Lane." She leaned forward to set her glass on the oblong coffee table in front of the sofa.

"Like the fact that he was superstitious on test days and had to wear the same outfit every day he had a test, right down to his underwear?"

Mia snorted. "Yeah. That."

"He numbered them."

"Tests?"

"Underwear. Permanent marker. That way if he got an

A on a test, he made sure to wear the same underwear for the next test."

"Are you kidding me?"

"No! For real." Savion held his hands up in surrender.

Mia shook her head, not sure she wanted any personal knowledge about Lane's underwear habits, past or present.

"So, what brings you to Phoenix for the holidays?" He moved, but only around the counter to sit on a bar stool.

"Mmm." Mia sipped her wine, put it back on the table, and stretched back on the sofa to get comfortable. "Well, my parents are traveling. They celebrated their thirty-fifth wedding anniversary before Thanksgiving, so they're in Greece. Since they're not around, my brother went to Texas with his girlfriend for the holidays. And my sister invited me to her place, but I don't like her in-laws."

"So, you chose to spend Christmas alone?"

"I have a few other friends in the area, so I have plans to see them. And we're planning a family holiday in January. Which will be cool, because we'll get to hear about Mom and Dad's trip."

He nodded, eyes on the tree.

"Are you married?" she asked him. Best to get that out of the way. Not that she seriously planned to sneak into the casita overnight and climb in bed with him. But it would be awkward sharing space with him over the holidays—even in a totally platonic way—and then to find out later that he was married with children.

And if someone with his body shape and big, kind eyes and sexy smile did fuel her fantasies for the next several nights, she would hate to learn he belonged to someone else. That was just wrong.

"Divorced."

"What brought you out here for Christmas?"

Savion emptied his glass and stood. "My ex-wife is getting remarried the day before Christmas Eve."

"You still love her?" Mia asked softly.

"No." His answer was simple and easily spoken. "But she and her fiancé took my kids to upstate New York with them to visit her family." When Savion met her gaze, Mia felt a pang of sadness for him.

"Can she do that?"

"She is their custodial parent, and I wasn't going to be the ass ex-husband who forbade her to take the kids on a vacation. Especially with the wedding."

Mia stewed over that for a moment.

"Do you see them?"

"Every other weekend." He reached for his keys and his phone. "Two weeks every summer. Blair's actually pretty good about letting me see them whenever I want. So, how could I say she couldn't have the kids at her wedding?"

Mia nodded. She got it. She had family and friends who had divorced, some amicably and some very much the opposite. Every family had a story, and every story had at least two sides, maybe more, depending on the kids. Still, it had to suck for Savion not to be with his kids over Christmas.

"How old are they?"

"My daughter is fifteen, and my son is eleven."

If Savion went to college with Lane, that put him in his mid-to-late thirties, depending on when he started school. Lane went straight to college from high school, but Mia knew that wasn't always the case. Some people took time off. Some high school graduates joined the military and then pursued their education.

She wanted to know more. She wanted to know if his kids liked his wife's new man. Why they had divorced. How long ago it happened. What Savion planned to do with his holiday vacation. Maybe she hadn't planned on sharing Toni and Lane's private paradise with anyone, but now that this guy was here, she was itching for conversation and company. Judging from the way he hedged backwards from the counter, he didn't feel the same way.

"Sure you don't need anything?"

She hadn't gone to the store yet. But she wasn't about to hand this guy a list of things to pick up for her, and she had no desire to leave the house right now. She could borrow from Toni's coffee supply again in the morning and make her way to the grocery store on her own.

"I'm going tomorrow," she told him.

"Going where?" He moved back into the heart of the room. "Leaving?"

"To the store," she corrected him with a laugh. "You should be so lucky that I would be leaving tomorrow."

"I'm kind of enjoying the company, if I'm being honest." His smile was harmless, but Mia saw his gaze slide over shoulders and then lower. Her nipples tightened at the heat in his eyes. As much fun as it had been to tease him a bit earlier, she sat forward now to take the strain off the shirt over her breasts. She wasn't particularly shy, but she had never done any full-frontal nudity for a total stranger, either. A few sips of wine had chased that boldness away.

She thought alcohol was supposed to work in the opposite direction. Then again, she wasn't a college kid anymore. She was an adult, and it had been a while since she dated anyone, and so, yeah, she felt a little out of her comfort zone at the moment.

"You don't wanna go now?"

Slowly, she stood and grabbed her glass from the coffee table. "Not really dressed for it," she mumbled as she joined him in the kitchen again.

"Probably not," he agreed. "And as much as I'd like your company, I would much rather you not change your clothes."

"This is weird." She poured more wine in his glass and then topped hers off. "Right? Is this weird?"

"I don't know," he admitted with a deep shrug. "I haven't been out in the world for a while."

"So, the divorce was recent?"

"No." He shook his head quickly. "No. Blair and I have been divorced for four years. But I work a lot. I see the kids a lot in the evening. Even if it's not my weekend, I watch them play ball or go to recitals." He settled on the stool again. "But I don't take the time for a social life."

"Which," Mia pointed at him with the hand holding the glass, "is probably a big part of why you're divorced."

Savion nodded. "Yeah, kind of."

"What do you do?"

"I'm a doctor." He propped his elbows on the counter and ducked his head to shove his fingers through his thick, dark hair.

"Mmm." She tipped her head. "So she knew going into your marriage that you would be a workaholic."

"She did. But there were other factors."

"I know." Mia sighed. "Takes two to tango and two to trip each other up and two to tear a marriage apart."

"Wow." He tilted his head enough to look at her. "Never heard it put that way."

"Do you want dinner? I'm hungry."

"You don't have to feed me. I can cook."

"Okay, so get up and help me fix dinner."

CHAPTER 3

SAVI

"So, why is this weird?"

Mia looked up from the orange bell pepper she was slicing.

"Will you start a list for me?" She ignored his question and glanced at the oversized Sub-Zero refrigerator as if she could see through the door. "I wanna make sure I get stuff to replace the food I'm stealing."

Savion picked up his phone with a grin.

"I will, but you might want to wait to replenish fresh produce," he reminded her. "Maybe pick it up right before we leave."

The second he said it, he regretted it. It just sounded wrong. Presumptuous, even though they were currently guests in Lane and Toni's home. He flicked his gaze up at her as he tapped the notes app on his phone. Mia didn't seem concerned by his choice of words.

"I know." She spoke quietly. "But I'll forget if I don't start keeping track. Put coffee on the list, too, please."

He added bell peppers and coffee, thought for a moment and tapped in brown rice, too.

"You didn't answer me." He moseyed over to the gas stove top and eyed the rice he had put on to boil.

"Why's it weird?" she asked. Savi turned when he heard the clatter of the knife on the counter, but Mia carried the cutting board to the stove and dumped the pile of fresh peppers, onions, and mushrooms into the hot skillet.

"Mm-hmm."

"It's a little weird for me, because I'm not usually one to parade around topless. And I've never been caught topless by a total stranger, and so, I've never had an ongoing conversation about being topless or braless with said total stranger."

He nodded when she glanced at him.

"I should apologize."

Mia set the cutting board down and reached for the spatula to flip the vegetables.

"For what?"

"I should have either let you know I was here the second I saw you, or I should have walked away and waited until...later...to let you know I was at the house."

She rested a hip on the counter and studied his face for a moment. Pink rushed her cheeks, but she grinned and finally gave him a half-hearted shrug.

"Did you like what you saw?"

"You know I did," he admitted. Odds were, he had seen the last of Mia's naked breasts, but what was the harm in telling the truth now?

"Well." She pursed her lips and laughed softly. "It's

been a long time since a guy's admired that view, so maybe it was kind of fun for both of us."

"No boyfriend back home?"

Savi hated to fish for information. It wasn't like he was going to hit on her. Make a move after they shared a dinner of stir-fry. Sneak into her room later tonight and watch her sleep or wake her with kisses. But damned if he wasn't going to be thinking about all of the above at some point later tonight, and it felt kind of sick to close his eyes and picture her out there by the pool if she had a boyfriend waiting somewhere for her to come back.

"No." She snorted. "My last boyfriend moved to some little industrial town in Ohio, I think. Married a chick named Jane."

"And what's wrong with Jane?" Savi kept his mouth still, trying to hide his amusement.

"Well, other than the fact that he was cheating with her, she's probably a size four, and she has incredible boobs. They have to be fake. But Todd let me know when he left how hot she was."

"Well, I'd be happy to take another look if you want me to, but from what I remember, Jane's got nothing on you."

Mia's laugh trilled through the room. Savi tuned in for a moment to hear "Have Yourself a Merry Little Christmas" playing around them. The tree lights sparkled in the corner, but the woman standing next to him was the true light. Her eyes were bright, and though her cheeks were pink again, she was still smiling, still laughing softly.

"You've never seen Jane," she reminded him.

"I don't need to," he answered. "And for the record, I like them real. Much more responsive to touch."

Mia stared at him for a moment and finally laughed out loud again.

"Wow. It's getting warm in here."

"The last woman I was with was a work fling. Lasted less than six weeks. And in that six weeks, we might have slept together a total of five times, and only one involved total nudity. Every other time was just shoving clothing aside and groping in a dark closet or office."

"No wonder I looked good to you," Mia mumbled. Savi watched her check the vegetables again. Noticing the rice was boiling, he set the timer on the microwave before turning back to her. "Anything might look good to a starving man."

"Even a starving man knows something special when he sees it."

He hadn't meant to say it out loud. In fact, he didn't realize he did say it out loud until Mia stopped moving, held the spatula still over the skillet, and eyed him with surprise. Their eyes met, but neither of them spoke. Savi wondered what she was thinking. Was she considering calling Toni to ask her or Lane to order him to leave? Or was she—like him—a little intrigued at the possibilities of what the two of them could find to do later?

Mia stirred, suddenly, shattering the moment. Of course, she wasn't interested in him. And even if she was, the most he could offer her was a seven-day fling in the desert and then a return to a dreary, cold Midwestern winter.

"I'm sorry." He shook his head and watched her turn the vegetables before setting the spatula down on the counter.

"For what?" She cleared her throat. "Are you apologizing for what I thought was a compliment?"

"Most definitely a compliment," he assured her, "but maybe out of line for me to say."

She shrugged. "Maybe it's out of line for me to enjoy it, but it's been a while since I've felt attractive, so I'm gonna go with the flow."

Savi laughed softly.

"Are you a vegetarian?" he asked when she took plates from the cabinet. Mia looked around for a moment and then met his eyes over her shoulder.

"No. Why do you ask?"

"I see rice and vegetables." He shrugged. "And it looks delicious, but I could have thrown some steaks on the grill."

Mia, one foot propped on the other again, pursed her lips as she turned the burner off under the rice.

"I'm kind of too tired to deal with it tonight," she said softly. "I'm sorry. I didn't think to ask you if you would want more."

"It's fine," he promised her. "But we might need more wine."

Mia glanced at the bottle, now nearly empty, and nodded.

"I only chilled one bottle." She nibbled on her lip and frowned at the refrigerator.

"Well, we could put another in the refrigerator now," he suggested.

"Good idea." Mia went back to dinner prep, and under her direction, Savi found a second bottle of Chardonnay in the pantry. He put it in the fridge and turned to find her plating their dinners.

"Do you enjoy cooking?" he asked her when she turned to him with a plate in each hand.

"Sometimes."

Savi splashed the rest of the wine in their glasses, careful to give her more, so she would have the chilled drink and when he needed a refill, he would be the one to get a warm pour.

"Dinner outside?" She tipped her head to the patio door. Savi snagged the glasses and followed her outside, purposefully leaving his phone on the counter.

He had talked to Lane for a few moments while Mia was in the shower. Lane had apologized profusely for the miscommunication with Toni. He offered to find Savi a room somewhere, but Savi told him he thought he and Mia were adults and could co-exist in the spacious living area for a week.

They could. Wouldn't have to be any different than two strangers bumping into each other or sharing space in a bed and breakfast or a hotel lobby or pool area. And yet, it already was. Savi hadn't intended to invite himself to dinner; he had only wanted to be polite and offer to pick anything up for her at the store.

Now he was drawn to her for more reasons than the two he had seen the second he walked into the house. He liked her. She was cute, a little bit feisty with a tiny little streak of vulnerability. He wanted to know more about her. Her favorite season. Favorite board game when she was a kid. If she'd ever been in love. Where she saw herself in ten years.

Joining her on the patio didn't mean they had to retrace their steps from earlier. No one had to take any clothing off, though his dick most definitely wanted to see more of Mia's skin. And curves. His dick wanted more than that, but Savi was an adult. He hadn't had a relaxing night like this with adult conversation and good food and wine in far too long. His phone—his main tie to his ex-wife and children—would be an unwelcome distraction.

CHAPTER 4

MIA

He wasn't so bad. She admitted it to herself later that night as she crawled into bed and turned the lamp off. Matt Dillon kept her company on TV, courtesy of *The Flamingo Kid* in Toni and Lane's stack of 80s movies, but her mind wandered back to her current housemate.

She and Savi had spent the entire evening on the patio. Mia had planned to talk to him over dinner and then come back inside for her book. She figured he would leave to go to the store, and maybe she would run into him tomorrow. Instead, they had finished their dinner, opened that second bottle of wine, and kicked back on the thick orange, yellow, and white striped cushioned lounge chairs.

Savion asked her what kind of work she did, and she answered, and that launched them into a philosophical conversation about children and education. Mia had been involved in the educational system in her Iowa hometown since she graduated from college. She taught for a couple of years, but she felt like she was doing more for the children in her district with her current position as a curriculum development specialist. She missed the one on one with the kids, but she loved working with teachers to identify learning objectives, assignments, and texts that would help students achieve more in their futures, too.

He asked her if she had children of her own. She didn't yet, but she wanted to, and she told him so. They talked about their childhoods, somewhat similar but still different. Mia had been the athletic type from the day she started walking, taking the T-ball field by storm when she was five. Savi told her his parents took him to tennis courts when he was younger, but he had no talent for the game. He had played flag football in middle school, but he'd given it up for band when he went to high school. Mia enjoyed literature classes and wiled away summer hours at the pool with library books. Savi only read nonfiction, and though he was a self-professed math and science guy, he told her he loved to read autobiographies and books about history.

But as they shared their stories, it became evident to Mia that they had both had a good childhood, and both of them were close with their families. Savi had asked about her siblings, and he laughed at the tales of her brother chasing her and her sister with frogs and snakes. Which, of course, made Mia suspicious enough to ask if he had tortured his sister in the same way. His ornery grin said everything he wouldn't when he invoked the 5th amendment.

Full dark pressed in around them, and still, they talked. Mia was still curious about his ex, about his kids, but other than asking if they liked school when they talked about her job, she didn't push for more details. Stretched out on the lounge chair, arms propped under his head, Savi looked exhausted and vulnerable and sexy all at once.

When that thought made its way through her body and throbbed in a few particular spots, she had decided it was time to get moving. Definitely best to say goodnight and go to bed. Alone. In the guest suite. The trouble with going to bed before he did was that she couldn't lock him out of the house.

She wondered about the fact that it didn't bother her anymore after they had only shared one evening together. For all she knew, he could still be a doctor by day and a dangerous man by night. He could sneak into the house while she was sleeping, but then again, she had locked the door to the suite, the lock was solid, and besides, Mia had always been a pretty good judge of character. And when she wasn't, it was more along the lines of trusting a guy to be faithful, not believing a guy was safe when he was actually a voyeur or a crazy, twisted maniacal killer.

They hadn't made plans for tomorrow. In fact, when Mia stood to come inside, Savi had blinked his eyes open and offered her a lazy smile. They said goodnight, and that was that. So why was she lying here in the dark thinking about him? About the pull of his shirt over his broad chest and shoulders? The thick wave of hair that wanted to swoop down over his left eyebrow. His olive-skinned-legs crossed at the ankles.

Mia wasn't a foot person, but his flip-flops forgotten at the side of the lounge chair and his bare feet on the lounge chair had struck her as intimate, sexy even. Right about now, she would love to slide her toes down his muscular calf and stroke them under the arch of his foot. If she were being greedy, she would like to touch a lot more of him than that. For instance, the underside of his forearms. Where he'd propped them behind his head. Her eyes had been drawn to his forearms time and again while they ate dinner. His fingers were bare. No tan lines from rings. No watch. Just dark hair on his olive skin and the lines of sinewy muscle under that skin.

She wanted to sink her teeth into his biceps, too, the delicious-looking bulges capped by his shirtsleeves. The ones that popped when he stacked his hands behind his head and stared up at the stars. She suspected he would taste like male, something woodsy or fresh, with maybe a hint of salt.

Thoughts of touching Savion followed her into sleep. Her dreams might have started with hints of Matt Dillon after watching the movie, but before long, the man in her arms had changed into the man she'd spent a perfectly innocent evening with. However, the dreams were anything but innocent.

In fact, her dreams left her hot and a little bit wet, and when morning rolled around and the sun falling through the slats of the shuttered windows woke her, Mia hesitated to get up. First, because she didn't want to jump back into reality where she and Savi were little more than polite strangers. Maybe if they stretched it, they could say they were now friends. And second, because Mia feared that one look at his face and the heat in the dreams would rush back, and Savi would look at her and just know she'd had inappropriate thoughts of him.

Still, even on vacation, she couldn't linger in bed all day. Not when there was coffee in the kitchen and a pool out there under that gorgeous sunshine. She thought for a moment about taking care of that desperate need those dreams had left her with, but she couldn't do it. Not with Savion somewhere on the premises. Finally, she climbed out of bed and headed straight to the restroom to take care of her morning business. No, she didn't usually brush her teeth just after using the bathroom and before making coffee, but she didn't usually share a kitchen with a man like Savi, either. And odds were, she reminded herself, she wouldn't see him anyway. Savi had his own kitchen, his own coffee maker, his own TV and living suite and stove and refrigerator and any other amenity Mia could think of in the casita. He wouldn't need to set foot inside the main house if he didn't want to.

She needed a shower but not before coffee. Instead, she stepped into a pair of soft knit shorts, tossed her nightshirt on the bed, and tugged on a loose gray sweatshirt. She slowed at the door and glanced back at the bed, considering a bra again. Still no real desire to put one on. Not when she was lounging around the house, though she would definitely wear one later when she left.

Her nipples perked up at the thought of running into Savi out there somewhere. Lucky for her, the sweatshirt was much looser than the shirt she'd worn around him last night. On the other hand, the shoulders were loose and wide and tended to slide off one side or the other. Mia glanced down at her shoulders, one at a time, decided no man would get turned on from a shoulder sticking out of a sweatshirt, and then backtracked to grab her phone.

The tree lights were off, though she had left them on for Savion when she left him out by the pool last night. But the kitchen lights were on, and she heard music. The flat screen TV on the wall was dark. Mia smelled coffee and breakfast cooking. So, he had ventured into the main house after all. She wondered how long he had been inside. If he had tiptoed to the closed and locked door of her guest suite.

"Good morning."

The smile he flashed at her dazzled like something out of a toothpaste commercial. Dressed in loose gray athletic shorts and a black T-shirt, bare foot again, Savi poured a mug of coffee and offered it to her.

"Thank you."

She should probably say something. Tell him she wasn't terribly comfortable with him being in the house when she was in the bedroom, unaware. But how could she when he'd only come inside to make coffee and apparently enough breakfast for both of them? Not to mention, it seemed hypocritical to complain about that when she was the one parading around either topless or braless. He hadn't done anything at all to make her uncomfortable. For all she knew, he was as into her as he was the fake Ficus in the corner of the dining room.

"Did you sleep well?" He turned his back to her to check whatever he was cooking on the stovetop.

"I did, thanks." She sipped her coffee and eyed his hard calves appreciatively. "You?"

"Fell asleep out by the pool." He shot her a sheepish grin over his shoulder. "Woke up after midnight. Pretty cold out there then. But yes, I did sleep well when I came back inside."

She wondered if he'd had any wild dreams, but she couldn't ask him that.

"I hope you like omelets." He stepped back from the stove and found the cabinet with plates.

"I do, but you didn't have to fix me breakfast."

"It was kind of nice last night." He cleared his throat. "Having dinner…"

Mia held her breath when Savi stole a quick glance at her. His eyes were dark and hot, and for a moment, she was certain they were thinking the same thing. He looked away suddenly, but the chemistry between them burned like sparks over her skin.

"Thought it would be fun to share breakfast," he finished. "Don't worry. I'm not gonna follow you around like a puppy. I'll be out of your hair when we're done."

Struck with thoughts of his long, elegant fingers in her hair and his nose nuzzling her cheek and her neck and maybe, his tongue flicking her earlobe and his teeth nipping her collarbone, Mia felt a flush of heat chase up her neck to her face. She took another drink mostly just to hide behind the bright orange mug.

"It was nice," she said as she turned away from him. "And I like puppies." She added the last in a small voice, but she knew from his soft snort that he heard her.

Savi used the spatula to slice through the huge omelet and then put a half on the plates he'd set side by side on the counter.

"Bell peppers and mushrooms and spinach."

"Sounds delicious." Mia's stomach growled on cue. A little embarrassed, she flicked her eyes up to look at him. He grinned, confirming that he'd heard it. She set her mug down on the island and pulled the refrigerator door open. "Juice?"

"Please."

Mia grabbed glasses and poured juice as Savi slid the plates over the counter. He took forks from the silverware drawer, she put the juice away, and they slid onto side by side bar stools.

"So, what are you going to do today?" she asked him.

"I don't know. I started the morning with a run."

"You what?"

"Went for a run." He shoved a heaping forkful in his mouth and watched her while he chewed.

"Wow." She grinned and nodded her approval. "I'm feeling like a slacker."

"It's how I relax."

"Running relaxes you?"

"Exercise." He shrugged. "At home I ride a bike."

"Figured you were a biker," she mumbled.

"How did you know?"

"Your legs."

Savi looked down at his legs with a frown. "What about my legs?"

"Your calves." Embarrassed to be called out for checking his legs out, Mia waved her hand absently in his general direction.

"What about my calves?" He stuck one leg out to look at his calf. Mia nearly moaned out loud when he bumped her, his skin warm against hers.

"They're very…" She licked her lips. "Muscular."

He met her eyes, clearly surprised by her comment.

"Have you been checking out my legs?" He tipped his head, feigning offense.

"No more than you were checking out my boobs last night."

"Show me a man who wouldn't have looked at your

breasts last night. Who wouldn't have liked what he saw so much that he kept looking, just to make sure you had actually covered them?"

"Show me a woman who doesn't look at a guy's legs." She shrugged. "I think it's cute that you call them breasts. Do you know how to talk dirty?"

"Is this a situation that calls for talking dirty? Sharing an omelet?"

Mia's cheeks flamed, but she laughed and started at him boldly.

"Just curious. Maybe your wife wasn't impressed with proper anatomical references when you were intimate."

Savi's eyes widened, apparently surprised that she'd gone there.

"My ex-wife hated the word *tits*," he admitted.

"Mm. So maybe she didn't like dirty talk?"

He hesitated.

"I'm sorry," Mia gushed. "Totally inappropriate for me to say."

Savi shook his head, looking more pensive than upset.

"Well, I thought she did." He narrowed his eyes in thought. "But maybe I was wrong about that, too."

"So, it was okay for you to say those kinds of words in the bedroom, but never outside of that?"

"Pretty much."

"What's she like?"

"Mmm. She's classy. She's a lawyer. Tall and thin and bossy."

Mia raised her eyebrows. "Well, at least your house-mate for the holidays is totally opposite."

"How so?"

"Well, I'm not a lawyer. I'm short and..." She patted her belly. "Curvy. Not bossy. And definitely not classy."

"I like curves," he told her, and as if to remind her that he'd seen some of hers, he dipped his gaze to her breasts and then looked up again. "And you have them in all the right places."

Mia rolled her eyes and forked another bite of the omelet.

"Do you like it?"

"The omelet?" she asked. "It's delicious."

"When a man talks dirty to you?"

She swallowed wrong, nearly choking on a mouthful of egg and gooey cheese and mushroom. Savi watched her, clearly amused, as she thumped her chest and reached for her juice.

"Wow."

"Too personal?"

Mia shrugged and laughed softly. "I guess I deserve it."

"Maybe." His slow smile chased a trail of heat low in her belly straight to her core. "And I do want an answer."

"Bossy," she mumbled. "Guessing you and your ex clashed a bit over that."

"In the end, we clashed over how to hold a pencil." Savi shrugged as if he couldn't care less. "Do you like dirty talk in the bedroom?"

"I like dirty talk anytime and anywhere."

"Good to know." He picked up his mug.

"Why's that good to know?"

Savi eyed her over the rim of his cup. "You're intriguing. I think I want to know everything about you."

"Intriguing? I'm intriguing?" Mia snorted. "I'm a plain Midwestern girl who got busted the first time in her life she was outside topless, thinking she would get a sexy tan before going back home to winter."

"I'm so happy I had the pleasure of being the one to bust you."

Mia ducked her head and covered her face with her hands.

"I think you're trying to kill me," he decided.

"How's that?"

"Parading around topless. Then with a tight T-shirt and no bra. Now the sweatshirt."

"What?" she yelped and dropped her hands. "It's way loose. You can't see anything."

"Except this."

Savi trailed his fingers over her shoulder, but his touch scorched her skin. Fire roared through her veins.

"My bare shoulder's gonna kill you?" She rested her elbow on the island and propped her forehead in her hand. "You poor guy. Has it been that long?"

"Mia, everything about you turns me on."

She tried to swallow, but her mouth was dry, her heart pumping at the base of her throat.

"I'm going to shower and go to the store." He finished his omelet and stood. "Do you wanna go with me?"

CHAPTER 5

Savi

He threw it out there, the invitation to tag along with him when he went to the store. Figured she would blow him off and go back outside to sit and catch some sun. Probably while wearing her bikini top this time. It was warm by their Midwestern standards, though Savion knew Lane and Toni would probably be decked in jeans if they were at home.

Mia surprised him, though. She blinked at him for a moment, finished her juice, and nodded.

"Yeah." She stood and grabbed her plate. "Yeah, I wanna go with you."

"Okay, good." He carried his plate to the dishwasher, watching Mia round the other end of the counter to do the same. "Meet you back here in fifteen?" Savi opened the dishwasher and ducked to put his plate inside.

She hesitated. "Um. Sure."

"Need more time?"

"Nope. That'll work." She leaned over to set her plate

on the lower rack. Her sweatshirt gapped in front, treating Savi to a peek at her gloriously naked breasts under the loose material. His dick was already poking at his athletic shorts from their conversation about talking dirty. Imagining hauling Mia's sweet little ass up on the island and sliding her sweatshirt over her shoulder to expose her breast. Telling her, as he ducked his head to flick her nipple with his tip of his tongue, that he wanted to spread her open and taste her pussy.

When she straightened, she brushed up against his front. Savi held his breath and stepped back. No need for Mia to know how hard he was. No sense in taking chances that he might embarrass himself if she rubbed a little too hard in one spot. Still, she looked at him as if she knew what he was thinking.

Or maybe as if she was thinking the same thing.

Savi cleared his throat and offered her a small grin. He was acting more like that nerdy math and science kid he used to be instead of the respected doctor he had become.

"Okay." She sounded breathless. Her soft voice lit a spark in his chest, sending heat through the rest of his body. Eyes locked with hers, he waited for her to make a move. Dangerously close to leaning in to hook her chin with his finger so he could tilt her face up for a kiss, Savion fought to control his own breathing. Mia's eyes dipped from his to his lips. He might have been an over-worked, under-socialized divorcee, but he was still a man.

He knew what it meant, the way her gaze lingered there on his lips. She was thinking about kissing him, too.

Not a good idea, he reminded himself. Because.

Because why?

He and Mia were complete strangers, yes, but they'd

hit it off last night. He had enjoyed hanging out with her, having dinner, relaxing by the pool. They were both single, available adults. Obviously attracted to each other. What harm could come from the two of them being intimate while on a holiday?

A rogue bubble of laughter broke loose from his lips. Judging from their conversation earlier, Mia would roll her eyes and laugh at him for that thought. If she liked it when a man talked dirty to her, odds were, she wouldn't think of something happening between them as being intimate.

Fucking.

What harm could come from the two of them fucking while they were on a holiday getaway?

"I'll…" She hesitated and flicked her gaze over his face again. "I'll meet you back out here in fifteen." She stepped back, breaking the spell.

"Sounds good." He nodded and turned, careful not to haul ass back to the casita. He was a grown man, for Christ's sake. A doctor. Friendly and fun and good in bed, if his lovers' reactions were honest. No reason to be afraid of what he was feeling or what Mia might be feeling. Intrigued or curious, yes. But no, he didn't need to *worry* about his attraction to her.

His cold shower didn't do much to take her off his mind, but he hustled through getting ready. Not just because the quicker he was back in the kitchen, the sooner he would see her again. Nope. He moved fast so he had no time to consider jerking off in the shower, Mia's face in mind.

When Mia joined him again, Savi was at the island counter with a book open in front of him. He had no idea what book it was. Sure, he'd packed it, thinking he would kick back by the pool and relax. But he'd packed a couple of books, and after getting ready to meet Mia, he'd grabbed the first one from his bag that he touched and carried it out to the island to wait.

His phone lit up with a text while he waited. One hand marking his page in the book—not that important as it was the preface—he pulled his phone over the counter with the other.

It snowed last night.

The text from his son brought a smile to his face. Damn, he'd been so caught up in Mia, he hadn't thought to call the kids last night. He would definitely call and talk to Aszia and Drew later this afternoon, but for now, he settled for a text.

How much did you get?

I think Mom said it was a foot.

Wow! Did you get outside?

Snowball fight with Micah.

Okay, that kind of soured his good mood. It shouldn't. Blair had every right to move on, to find love with someone else. Savi hoped one day he would find love with someone else. And yes, if he did, he hoped his children would be close to her, just the same as he was glad the kids liked Micah.

But that didn't mean sharing them didn't sting.

Did Aszia go out, too?

She and Mom made cookies.

Another sucker punch in his gut. Again, not that he wanted to be with Blair. But the homey image of his ex with his kids, baking cookies, doing holiday things sucked the life out of him. He and Blair were over, and mostly, they were friends, now. Friendly enough to coparent, at least. Thank God, Savi had good relationships with his kids. If there was bad blood between them, it would really hurt to spend the holidays so far away from them, while they lived it up in snow and Christmas lights and home-made cookies with Blair and her new love.

"Ready?"

Savi pushed away the negative energy and closed his book. Mia's small smile was almost enough to make him feel good again. But dammit, he missed the kids.

"What're you reading?" Mia moved closer to the island. Savi eyed her messy ponytail, still a bit damp from her shower. No makeup other than lip gloss, as if her lips hadn't looked delectable enough without it. "*An American Life.*" Mia tipped her head to the side and shrugged.

"You're not a Reagan fan?"

"Reagan's fine," she looked at him with a quick grin, "but I read thrillers."

Mia stood so close to him, Savi could feel the heat from her body. She smelled fresh and clean, something simple compared to the high dollar perfume his ex used to wear. He liked it. In fact, he liked it so much, he had a sudden urge to taste her. Not just a kiss. He wanted to gather her in his arms and drag his tongue up the back of her neck. Sink his teeth into her shoulder and draw a gasp or a moan from her plump, glossy lips.

"You ready?" He shoved his chair back out of his way to stand. The loud barking noise of the legs on the tile jarred him, but that was for the best. If they didn't get out of the house soon, Savion might go full caveman on Mia and throw her over his shoulder to carry her to his bedroom. Better yet, he could simply press her up against the nearest wall and slide her skimpy blue shorts down to drive into her right there.

"So what's wrong?" she asked as he followed her out the front door.

Worried that his facial expression had just broadcasted his thoughts, Savi simply arched his brows when she glanced at him over her shoulder.

"Nothing. Why?"

"You looked a little down back there. In the kitchen."

Oh. Okay, that he could talk about.

"Drew texted me." He pulled the door closed, jiggled the fancy chrome handle to make sure it was locked, and they headed down the front walk to his rented Range Rover in the driveway.

"Your son."

He nodded.

"Everything okay?"

Again, Savi nodded, but once they were both in the SUV, he had to say more. He couldn't cut off a normal conversation like this, because his head—both of them—would go right back to inappropriate thoughts about the woman beside him.

"Well, it snowed. Blair says maybe a foot."

"Blair is your ex?" When Savion nodded, Mia angled her whole body toward him. "Did you talk to her?"

"No. Drew said Blair's guess was a foot. He and Blair's fiancé had a snowball fight."

"Well, that sucks," she mumbled. At his snort, she flinched and looked up at him with wide eyes. "Sorry. It doesn't. You want him to have fun."

"I do," Savi agreed. "I just wish…"

"You were there having fun with him."

Savi started the Range Rover, but he didn't put it in gear. Mia was watching him closely when he glanced at her.

"No. Not there. I just wish I could be with the kids. For Christmas."

"Of course, you do." Her words, her voice, was gentle, comforting. "Tell me about them."

"The kids?"

"Yes."

"Um. Drew's a card shark."

"Yeah?"

"The kid could win the world series of poker."

"Who taught him to play?"

"Blair's dad."

"That's pretty funny."

"Yeah, until he's fifteen, and he's at a party where they decide to play strip poker. He'll have all kinds of girls stripped down to nothing."

"Well, then he'll have fun," she said with a giggle.

"Not what I wanted to hear," Savi muttered. He put the SUV in reverse and backed out of the drive.

"What about your daughter?"

"Aszia is into photography. She's on the school paper."

"Really? She's a sophomore?"

"Yes. Pretty awesome seeing her photo creds."

Mia smiled sweetly. "Does she play poker?"

"Hell no." Savi reached over the console of the SUV and fake punched Mia's leg.

"I'm teasing."

"I wouldn't have known what to do with a naked girl when I was fifteen," he admitted. He slowed at the ornate gate at the entrance to the neighborhood and watched it creep open.

"Really?" Mia tipped her head at him.

"Well, I might've had ideas, but I would have embarrassed myself."

She snickered, but when Savi looked her way again, she was looking out her window.

"I was nineteen when I learned the ropes," she told him. "I was busy with school stuff. Friends. Softball. Didn't have time for boyfriends or hook ups."

"And I was too busy studying."

"Was your wife your first?"

"No." Savi laughed heartily. "No. I slept with a girl from my anatomy class when I was eighteen."

"Uh huh. Studying, right?"

"Something like that."

"How'd it go?"

"You want the truth?"

"You said you were a math and science guy."

"I don't know what that means in regard to the question. But I don't think I lasted five minutes, so I embarrassed myself anyway."

Mia grinned. "If you were some athletic stud or biker or something, you would have lied to me and said it was fantastic."

"Oh, it was fantastic." He nodded. "Maybe not for her, but I enjoyed the hell out of it."

"Guys." Mia rolled her eyes.

"What about your first time? Fantastic?"

"Probably for the guy I was with, sure."

"But not you?"

"No. In fact, I was so underwhelmed by it, that I waited another year before I tried it again."

"And how was that time?"

Mia dropped her head back to rest on the seat.

"This store okay?" Savi hitched a thumb to his left to indicate a large whole food market. Mia rolled her head his way and nodded.

"It's fine," she said quietly. "And my second experience wasn't that much better than my first."

"Well, that sucks."

"You're telling me."

"But you've had better experiences since then? Right?"

"I suppose."

"Mia, can you orgasm during sex?"

She stared at him blankly. Savi watched the rush of red in her cheeks. He couldn't believe he had asked her such a personal question, and yet, why not? Weren't people a lot more open about these things these days?

"No. Not often." She blinked and looked away.

"But." Savi parked the silver SUV and turned to look at her. "You can get there? On your own?"

Mia roared with self-conscious laughter. She dropped her head forward to hide her face in her hands and groaned out loud.

"Did you really just ask me if I can get myself off?"

"I did." He laughed softly.

"Oh my God."

"Well, I mean, you should enjoy sex. If you don't, there might be a medical reason. Or it might be a prescription—"

"Are you an ob-gyn?"

"No, I'm in palliative care."

Mia flinched again. "Oh God. How in the hell can you do that? That's gotta be a horribly difficult practice."

He answered with a curt nod. "It can be. It can also be rewarding."

Mia shivered.

"You haven't answered my question."

She huffed out a long, exasperated sigh and nodded.

"Yes, I can orgasm. It just doesn't happen often with a partner."

Savi studied her pink cheeks for a moment, and finally he narrowed his eyes and tipped his head.

"Okay."

"Okay?" she repeated. "Okay? What does that mean?"

"It can mean anything you want," he answered simply. "But mostly, I'm just happy to hear that."

CHAPTER 6

MIA

He was happy to hear that? He was—what? Why? Why would it matter to Savion Merchant if she could reach orgasm when she had sex? Or touched herself? Savi climbed out of the SUV and swung the door closed without a backwards glance. Mia stared after him, mouth agape, shocked by the direction their conversation had taken.

Then again, maybe she shouldn't be. They'd talked about talking dirty during sex, right? But still. Savi Merchant, drop-dead gorgeous perfect stranger turned maybe-friend, had come right out and asked her if she could orgasm.

Mia scrambled out of the passenger seat and hurried after him. She caught up to him as he neared the automatic entrance of the market. Savi shot her a toothy grin as the door opened.

"What—? Why did you ask me that? Why would you be happy to hear that I can—" Mia caught herself before she blurted the word out. A mom with two grade school-aged children eyed them as Savi grabbed a shopping cart. "You know."

"Why would I be happy to hear that you can *you know*?" he asked as they strolled through the produce department. "What are we doing for dinner tonight?"

Mia, still flustered over the conversation about sex, caught her breath and blinked at him. Dinner tonight. Savi wanted to have dinner again tonight?

"Well, I mean," he shook his head, "if you have other plans, it's fine. I was just wondering if we should get some fresh produce now and use it. And then get more later, before we leave."

She liked the sound of that. That Savi had said *we*. Maybe they were only flirting, playing around, but being here with him made her feel deliriously happy for the moment. Maybe for now that was all that mattered.

"I don't," she said softly. "Have other plans."

Their eyes locked, and finally, Savi nodded. He tore his gaze from hers and examined a bell pepper.

"Homemade pizza?" he suggested.

"Sure."

"What do you like on your pizza?"

"Um." He still hadn't answered her. About why it mattered to him that she could enjoy sex. That she could reach climax and get off when she touched herself. How in the hell was she supposed to concentrate on pizza toppings? "Green peppers. Pineapple. Sausage."

"Pepperoni?"

"Sure."

"You are an incredibly sexy woman, Mia," he said quietly as he perused the selection of green peppers. "I'm glad you can make yourself come if your lovers aren't good enough to do it for you."

Again, Mia stood and watched him, stunned by what he had said. By the intensity in his voice. Savi strolled further down the aisle and stopped by the mushrooms. He held up a package and turned to her, eyebrows arched in question.

"Yes."

He nodded and kept moving. How in the hell was he playing this so cool? For God's sake, she was ready to tear his clothes off and push him up against the cooler of specialty water on the endcap to have her way with him. Either that or snag a few bottles of the chilled water and pour it over herself to put out her fire.

"Why is this fair?" She hurried after him and snatched at his shirtsleeve. Savi turned from the pineapple he was now studying.

"What?"

"Why do you get to quiz me about my sex life?"

"I'm not. Just making sure you can enjoy it. If not during sex, at least when you pleasure yourself."

Mia blinked at him, too stunned to even think about hiding her face when she blushed.

"What about you?"

"What? Do I enjoy sex? Or can I pleasure you? Make you come?"

"Savi!" Mia gasped. "You can't—you can't say that!"

"Why not?"

"To me! You can't say that to me!" Her voice jumped up an octave, and her belly did a freefall. She liked what he had said. She liked it. She liked him. And dammit, if she didn't want him to touch her right here, right now. "Here! You can't say that stuff here!"

"But I can back at Lane and Toni's house?"

"Can? You can say it back at their *house*?"

"I *could* say it," he nodded, "or I could *do* it."

This time, Mia's mouth snapped shut. She stared at Savi mutely, her stomach buzzing with nerves and anticipation and arousal. How had they gone from discussing what his wife, his kids were like to—to—THIS?! Okay, sure, there had been a short conversation about talking dirty, but an hour ago, this guy seemed more likely to discuss molecular biology than to say the word *tits*. Now it sounded like he was propositioning her in the produce department in the grocery store.

"Are you offended?" He turned back to the pineapples, selected one, and set it in their cart, speaking so quietly, Mia had to lean into him to hear him.

"No!" She rushed to answer him.

"No?" He tipped his head to study her face for a moment.

Mia was definitely not offended. Interested. She was more than interested, but still, she couldn't get past the fact that they were in the grocery store with other shoppers milling about.

"Not at all."

"Okay."

When he pushed the cart away without further comment, she followed him. Her insides were still a jumbled mix of need and nerves, all coiled tightly, ready to spring loose at the okay signal from Savi. Not that she had any idea what that signal might be.

They purchased some snacks. A bag of chips. Some

crackers and cheese. Savi led her into the alcohol aisles, and she watched him select a cab. Nodded mutely when he held it out for her inspection.

Once they were satisfied with their haul, they joined the line at the registers, making small talk as if they hadn't had a sexual conversation just minutes ago. Mia rattled, shared her opinion about the Kardashians, ignoring the sexy fit of Savi's low hung khaki shorts. The way his shirt stretched over his shoulders, drawing attention to his slim waist, too. He'd seen her topless; didn't seem fair that she was left to imagine what his bare chest looked like. Muscled, for sure. Judging from the look of his legs, probably ripped. Would he have hair on his chest? A happy trail arrowing down into the waistband of the shorts that kept drawing her eye? Tattoos?

Savi paid for the groceries with a card. Mia tried to argue, tried to divide things up at the conveyor belt. He insisted they could settle up later. She felt guilty for standing there watching him insert his card and sign the screen, but she would have felt silly arguing about it in front of the checkout clerk.

"Too bad we have cold groceries," he said once they were back in the SUV. She buckled her seatbelt and watched him from under her lashes.

"Why?"

"We could've found something to do." He sent her an innocent shrug. "Driving range. We could go hiking. Bike ride."

She grinned. It all sounded fun. Mostly because it would involve spending time with him. She wasn't a golfer, but she didn't hate the idea of Savi standing behind her with his arms around her, trying to show her how to swing a club. She wouldn't mind a bike ride or a hike, though she wasn't dressed for either.

Not to mention, if they were going to go with physical activities, Mia could think of a few other things she would rather do with Savion Merchant. Riding him reverse cowboy would be a fun place to start.

"We could always take the groceries home and then do something."

Like make out by the pool.

Mia bit her lip to keep her mouth shut. Savi pursed his lips as if he was considering finding something to do after they put the groceries away. She looked away before she could laugh out loud at the possibility of his thoughts mirroring her own.

"We could," he said, though he sounded anything but excited at the thought now. He nodded, though, as if that settled it, leaving Mia to wonder what exactly he was thinking.

At the house, they both wrestled reusable bags filled with groceries into the house and danced around each other to put their purchases away. While Mia was completely at ease with him, though she liked being around him, there was none of the sexual tension between them from earlier. It was as if getting back into the SUV to drive back here had flipped a switch and thrown Savion back to being that quiet, mild-mannered guy who had been flustered to find her topless out on the patio.

Once the groceries were put away, Savi excused himself to call his kids. Mia appreciated that he wanted to be in contact with them, but she hated to see him slip into the casita, leaving her alone. How had she become attached to him so quickly?

Reminding herself she had come to Toni and Lane's to relax, not to follow some guy around like a lovesick puppy, she found her book in the guest suite and went outside to read by the pool. She wasn't a terribly picky reader, at least not with her genre, but she did have favorite authors.

Probably should be reading a Christmas romance, something cozy and sexy, someone snowed in way up north for the holidays. The thought brought a smile to her face as she relaxed on the lounge chair and opened her thriller to her saved page.

She wasn't sad about being here for Christmas—especially not now, not after meeting her housemate—but she had to admit she sort of missed the cold and the hustle and bustle back home. While Toni and Lane's Christmas tree was pretty, something about stepping out onto the patio and sitting outside in shorts—topless just yesterday—put a damper on the Christmas spirit.

CHAPTER 7

Savi

"What're you doing out there, Dad?"

Savi flopped backwards on the bright green sofa in the casita living room. He was torn between wanting to keep Mia—her existence and the fact that she was here—to himself and hating to lie to his kids. There was no reason to keep Mia a secret. He hadn't snuck away to Arizona to rendezvous with a woman for a sexy holiday romp. He'd come here for a vacation. To find something to do with himself since his kids were with Blair and Micah. But there was no reason to tell them about Mia, either. Sure, he already considered her a friend, and they could easily stay in touch once the holidays were over. But his friendships didn't have to involve the kids, especially not long-distance friendships.

He sure as hell couldn't tell Drew that he had just talked about sex and orgasms in the produce aisles of a grocery store with Mia. That he had flirted outrageously to throw Mia off-guard, to make her blush, but the joke had been on him, because suggesting to Mia that he could say things like that to her or just do them to her had made his dick hard as steel., and that erection was still poking at the zipper of his shorts.

"Just went to the grocery store and picked up a few things to snack on," he told Drew.

"Did you get those new chips we like?"

He hadn't, because they were greasy and only Drew liked them, and anyway, he bought cheese and crackers and wine to share with Mia. They could sit out by the pool and have a glass of wine before he made pizza.

"No."

"Did you go swimming?"

"No."

"But it's warm there, isn't it?"

"It's really nice here," Savi agreed. "But I'm sure the pool water is pretty cold."

"So you just went there to get groceries?" Drew sounded puzzled. "You should have just come to New York to Mom's wedding."

Savi pinched the bridge of his nose. That was the last damned place he wanted to spend his holidays. Not that he would be welcome there anyway. He and Blair did well with communication now, better than when they were married, but no, she wouldn't want him at the wedding. Savi doubted Micah would want him there, and he knew Blair's parents didn't want to see him.

"I'm here with a friend," Savi heard himself say. So much for keeping his mouth shut about Mia.

"Oh. That's cool." Drew's tone suggested he definitely approved of Savi hanging out with a friend for Christmas. "Which friend? What's his name?"

"Her name is Mia," Savi answered.

"You have a girl friend?

"She's not my girlfriend," Savi corrected him, though his dick throbbed in disagreement. "Just a friend. We had dinner together and sat by the pool last night."

There was a tussle on the other end of the line, and then Savi heard the phone being passed around.

"You have a girlfriend?" Aszia asked him. In the background, he could hear Drew griping about his sister stealing the phone from him.

"No. Just a friend."

"Is she pretty?"

"Aszia." He sighed, angry with himself for letting it slip about Mia being here.

"Just a question."

"Yes, she's pretty."

"Cool."

"What're you guys doing?" Savi asked the question in an attempt to head off any further questions about Mia.

"We're all gonna go for a walk in the snow," Aszia told him.

Savi felt a pang of regret and reminded himself that he would get his fair time with the kids. Of course, they should be with Blair and Micah for their big day. But why did their big day have to be right before the biggest holiday of the year?

"Has it snowed more?"

"I think we got four more inches."

Savi heard a deeper male voice holler something on Aszia's end of the line.

Aszia sighed.

"I have to go," she told him. "Mom wants to talk to you."

Savi squeezed his eyes closed, knowing it would be useless to argue that he didn't need to talk to his ex-wife.

"You're in Arizona with a woman?"

He flinched at Blair's greeting.

"And you thought it would be a good idea to share that with your son?"

"I am not here with a woman," he mumbled on a tired sigh.

"Is there or is there not a woman named Mia there with you?"

"There is a woman here named Mia," he admitted. "She's Toni's friend. I guess Toni and Lane got their wires crossed about who was staying here."

"Hmm." Blair sounded snippy. "How fortuitous for you."

Savi rolled his eyes. "Not that there's anything going on, but what difference would it make to you if there was? Aren't you marrying the love of your life in a few days?"

This time Blair sighed.

"You're right. I just wish you would have told me you were with someone. Instead of telling Drew."

"Blair, I didn't know she would be here until I walked into the house." Savi decided it would be best to keep those details to himself. "I only told Drew I was with a friend because he was worried about me and saying I should have come with you guys to the wedding."

Blair laughed softly.

"Is she pretty?"

Because the hard edge melted from her voice, he answered her this time.

"Yes, she is."

"Then loosen up and have some fun, Savi. For God's sake, you didn't do it with me."

He hung up a moment later with promises from the kids via Blair that they would send pictures of their walk in the snow. But Blair's last words didn't sit well with him; he resented her suggesting that they hadn't had fun together. Sure, things had gone wrong, but they'd had a few good years first.

The house was empty. Tree lights on, but no music playing. Savi found Mia on the patio, curled up on a lounge chair with a book. She hadn't seen him yet, so he ducked back into the casita to grab his book on Ronald Reagan and joined her outside.

"Would it be wrong to say I prefer the outfit you had on yesterday when I came outside?"

Mia rested her head on the chair and snorted.

"No. You're never gonna let that go, are you?"

"No. In fact, I'm pretty sure you and I are gonna exchange numbers and stay friends, and when we're old and gray, I'm gonna text you and say remember that time…"

The grin on her face told him she was okay with his teasing.

"At that time, I'm gonna wish you had taken a picture to send me. My tits'll probably be saggy and gross by then."

"I already wish I had taken a picture."

He felt her gaze on him, so he closed his book and stared back at her.

"You could just ask me to take my shirt off again," she suggested.

"And would you?"

"Maybe." She shrugged.

Savi looked around the patio, the private backyard. Of course it was private, or she wouldn't have taken her top off yesterday. Still. Blair's final words to him echoed in his head. He wanted to have fun with Mia. But sitting here like this, both of them with a book to relax with, was fun. Getting groceries with Mia was fun. Then again, that was mostly because he'd boldly proclaimed that he could make her come.

But no matter what he did or didn't do with Mia, he didn't want it to have anything to do with Blair. Or what Blair had suggested.

"So, if I said, *God, Mia, I'd love it if you took your top off*," he tipped his head, "you might take your shirt off and sit here with me?"

"I might."

Savi licked his lips and nodded.

'Is that a yes? You want me to take my shirt off?"

"I do." He grinned. "I really want you to take your shirt off."

Mia hesitated a moment longer. Savi thought he had called her bluff, that she would blush and laugh and duck her head and say no. To his surprise, she closed her book and set it between her legs, and then gathered the tail of her T-shirt in her hands. She eased the material up, exposing her flat belly inch by inch. Savi's chest was tight with a breath he couldn't remember how to take.

She peeked at him, a look of mischief on her face, as a stripe of pale pink lace came into view.

"I've never..." She arched her eyebrows. "Taken my clothes off for a stranger."

Clothes.

The word was like a lightning bolt at the base of his cock.

"You're doing great," he promised.

"Yeah?"

"Yes."

She laughed, and THERE was that blush. A much deeper, furious pink than the lace cups that covered her breasts. Savi wasn't sure what he liked more at the moment. The smile on her face and the fiery teasing in her eyes or the blush in her cheeks. Or the perfectly round globes of her breasts as she pulled her shirt up and over her head.

The blush darkened, but Savi's eyes slid lower to her bra as she dropped her T-shirt. The creamy curves over the top of the lace cups made his body vibrate with need.

"If it makes you feel any better," he told her, "I've never sat and watched a stranger take her shirt off like that."

"No?" She picked her book up.

"Nope."

"Okay."

When Mia opened her book to read, Savi did the same. As if he could fucking concentrate with Mia not even a foot away, only soft pink lace holding her breasts. A quick peek treated him to her right nipple pressed into the lace.

"Mia?"

"Hmm?" She kept her eyes on her book.

"Can we not be strangers?"

"What"

"Maybe we could be friends? Instead of strangers?"

"We're friends." She nodded.

"After all, we cooked together last night."

"Right." She shrugged and grinned.

Savi turned his attention back to his book long enough to read three more words.

"Mia?"

"Hmm?"

"What if I asked you to take your bra off?"

She quirked an eyebrow, but she put her book down without a word.

"Do you want me to?"

"Fuck yes."

"Dr. Merchant, did you just say the word fuck?"

He grinned and wagged his eyebrows.

"I did."

"I kinda liked it," she confessed. Savi's cock throbbed as Mia leaned forward and reached back to unhook her bra. Feeling a bit like a pig, but not enough to care, he leaned forward for a better view. Her fingers gave the hook an expert twist, and the elastic eased. Savi took a long moment to admire her hands, her delicate wrists and bare, but perfectly shaped fingernails. She shimmied her shoulders, drawing his attention to the smooth expanse of her back and her perfectly rounded shoulders.

She tipped her head forward and her hair fell, hiding her face from his eyes. He fought a sudden urge to fist her locks around his hand and sink his teeth into her neck. Drag his tongue down her spine.

Savi dipped his gaze lower to the waistband of her shorts. Imagined cupping her sweet little ass cheeks in his hands.

Mia tipped her head back as she slipped the pink straps down over her arms. She met his eyes as the lace fell to her lap.

"This is crazy," she whispered. Savi watched her relax back against the lounge chair again, his hungry eyes roving over the muscle in her upper arm, the flat of her belly, the lace cups now pooled in her lap, and finally, her bare breasts. Eyes closed, she balled her fingers into fists and pressed her lips together.

"Are you nervous?" Savi's heart pounded up his throat, and his dick perked up again when Mia's nipples tightened under his gaze.

"Um. Maybe?"

"Relax, Mia." He spoke quietly. "I'm not gonna jump you."

"Okay." She nodded, eyes still closed. "It just feels...weird."

"Weird bad or good?"

Savi watched her rub her lips together for a moment. She blinked and turned to look at him.

"Good."

"You're beautiful."

Mia groaned and laughed as she crossed her arms over her chest.

"Are you cold?"

"No," she said around a laugh. "It's just knowing that you're looking at me."

"I can promise to behave," he assured her, "but I can't promise not to look."

"Well, that's kind of the point of me undressing, isn't it? So you can look?"

"How about a glass of wine?"

"Gonna ply me with alcohol to loosen me up?"

"I don't plan to ply you with alcohol, no, but maybe a glass of wine would make you feel more comfortable."

"Maybe," she agreed.

"I'll be right back." He scooted to the edge of the chair to stand.

"I'll go with you."

Savi watched her slide to the end of the lounger, his eyes locked on the sway of her breasts. As she stood, she looked up and caught him staring. Rather than cover herself this time, she only laughed, let the blush climb in her cheeks. Savi stepped aside to follow her, his eyes taking a long, slow stroll over the tiny swell of her hips and her long, lean legs. With her back to him, he adjusted his cock, though nothing but driving balls deep into Mia's pussy was going to relieve the ache.

"Do you want a snack?" she asked when they were both inside. Savi found the wine bottle opener and went to work on the cork.

Did he want a snack? Maybe a lick of her nipples with a side of something hot and wet.

Blair would be stunned if she could read his mind. While their sex life had been satisfying, he wasn't sure he had ever felt this wild need, this outrageous hunger, for his ex. For a moment, he considered sitting Mia up on the counter and feasting on her breasts. Circling her hard pink nipples with his tongue. Nuzzling the curves of her breasts, the extreme dip between them, with his nose and his tongue. Scraping his teeth over her sensitive skin.

Biting her.

Kissing her to make it better.

"Sure." Impressed that his voice sounded normal, and not like his balls were seventeen shades of violent purple and blue, he uncorked the bottle and watched her find the slab of aged cheddar in the refrigerator. For a few moments, they worked in silence, preparing a snack to take out by the pool. Savi poured the wine while Mia sliced the cheddar and arranged the slices on a wooden board. She disappeared into the pantry and returned in a moment with the crackers he chose.

Once the snack board was arranged to her liking, Savi stepped closer to her. Mia froze at the counter, eyes still on the cheese and crackers. Savi was close enough that his knee bumped her leg. The feel of her soft, warm skin against his made his heart slow, each furious pound hammering in his throat and his ears.

"Mia."

She flattened her hands on the counter, as if to steel herself for whatever he was thinking, and then lifted her chin to look at him.

"What?"

"Is this okay?" He let his eyes slide over her lips and down to her breasts. Her nipples were soft and relaxed now, making him wish he could sleep with her and wake with her in his arms. That he could wake her, rouse her with his hands, his mouth.

She nodded.

"If I'm making you uncomfortable—"

"You're not," she assured him. "But I want you to touch me."

Rather than answer her, Savi traced his fingertips over her shoulder and down her arm. He linked his fingers with hers and leaned in until she turned to face him. His vision from moments ago was back. Throwing Mia up on the counter to explore her heat and her curves. But he also remembered what she'd said about not orgasming during sex, with a partner, and he wanted to spend today worshipping her body, for her pleasure. Not just his.

He looked, though. Mia eyes were dark and intense with need, and her teeth worried her full lower lip, and as his gaze slid lower to the curves of her breasts, her nipples perked up again. Savi trailed the fingers of his free hand around her waist, tracing the top of her shorts. Mia jumped; her soft gasp of surprise or delight went straight to his head. The little one that throbbed with appreciation.

"You're so fucking beautiful." He let go of her hand to cup her cheek. The honesty, the open communication, saying what he was thinking felt good. Even after Blair, when Savi dated or engaged in sexual relationships of any kind, he felt bound to his reputation. He carried his professionalism with him everywhere. He didn't want to use Mia for his pleasures, but he wanted to be free, to be himself, as he loved her. For her sake, as well as his own.

Mia's parted lips beckoned him. He smoothed his thumb over the corner of her mouth, fighting the desire to haul her against his body and grind his cock into her middle. Maybe later. Right now, he wanted sweet, soft kisses with her. He wanted to stroke his tongue over hers, to learn her taste, the texture of her tongue, her skin. He wanted to go slow, to hear the shift in her breathing when he did something she liked. To make her whisper his name, to need more.

He wanted to fuck Mia in every damned position known to man, and he was game to make up new ones. But right now, this moment, this was for Mia. He had told her he could make her come. He wanted to make her scream with pleasure and lust and desperation for more.

He watched her eyes close as he leaned in closer to kiss her. The soft blue was gone, but Savi found himself fascinated by the curl of her lashes on her cheek. The trust she felt if she could stand here, topless—nearly naked—with her eyes closed and her lips parted to receive his kiss when she'd just met him yesterday.

Savi kissed her. A barely there kiss on the corner of her mouth, his lips chasing the path his thumb had taken only a moment ago. She was quiet, but he felt it already, a slight hitch in her breath. He made another pass, his closed lips full over hers, and then again, a soft, curious kiss. Her lips soft and warm under his. Hovering there, he dragged his knuckle down over the slope of her breast and nudged her nipple.

"Savi," she moaned softly. She wanted more, and his cock wanted more, but he wasn't ready to give into her yet. He wanted to tease her, to drive her need high and hard before giving her more.

When he didn't touch her again, she opened her eyes.

"Why aren't your eyes closed?" Her words feathered over his lips.

"Because I want to see you," he told her, rubbing his lips over hers. "I don't wanna miss a second of looking at you."

"You said you could make me come."

"And I can." He nodded.

"I need—"

"What?" He flicked his tongue over the center of her upper lip. "What do you need, Mia?"

"I need you to touch me." She stared at him with intense heat. "This is crazy, Savi, but the things you said to me earlier—"

"Not yet." He lifted his hand to brush her hair back from her face.

"Please."

Savi groaned when she moved closer, when she cupped his cock through his shorts.

"I want this."

Savi stepped back when her fingers went to his zipper.

"Not yet."

"Savi—"

Before she could say more, he plunged his tongue into her mouth to sweep deep and tangle with hers. She kissed him back, met his tongue thrust for thrust. Savi moved his hand to cup the back of her neck and angle her mouth so he could deepen the kiss. With their lips locked, he explored her teeth, the roof of her mouth, and back to her tongue. Mia's hands were suddenly on his shoulders, her fingers digging painfully, her middle pressed to him, a soft, warm place to grind his hungry cock.

"Mia." He eased her back just enough to look her in the eyes.

"You want this, too." She narrowed her eyes at him.

"Fuck yes, I want this." He licked her lips. "I wanna go caveman and drag you to my bed and spread your legs and bury my cock inside you and never get out of bed until we fly home."

"Then do it," she urged him. "Do me."

"I can't." Part of his plan, but at the moment, with his dick painfully hard and his balls black and blue, he cursed himself.

"What? Why not?" Mia leaned into him again. This time, Savi felt her breasts on his chest.

"No condoms."

"Are you fucking kidding me?" She dropped her head back and squeezed her eyes closed. "All those things you said to me, and you didn't get any condoms when we were at the store?"

"Today is going to be all about you," he told her. Her frown eased a bit as he smoothed the palm of his hand down over her back. "I told you I could make you come, and I intend to do just that. I'm gonna make you scream and sob my name, and then I'm gonna do it again and again and again."

She blinked and stared at him with wide, hungry eyes.

"Promise?"

"I promise."

"This is all I want for Christmas. This. Right now. With you."

Savi stepped back and reached for a glass of wine. She took it when he handed it to her, sipped from it when he nodded at it.

"Savi?" She pressed her lips together.

"Take another drink," he urged her. When she did, he took the glass from her, set it aside, and kissed her again. Mouths open this time, their tongues danced and stroked. Savi loved the taste of her cab. Maybe he would pour it over her breasts and lick them clean.

"I like kissing you," she whispered.

"I love the way you taste." Savi cupped her ass in his hands, a thrill shooting through him when she lifted her legs and locked her ankles around his waist.

"What're you doing?"

Mia looked around as he sat her on the counter and eased her back a bit.

"Kiss me with your eyes open," he dared her.

CHAPTER 8

MIA

Savi rested his hands on her thighs, and he pushed them apart enough to step into the V between them. Still with that ferocious ache inside, the need for him to put his hands on her, to fill his hands and play with her nipples, Mia cupped his face in her hands and leaned close to kiss him.

With her eyes open. Watching him watch her sent heat rushing through her body, straight to her core. His dark eyes were hot with lust, but there was more. Savi was a good man, compassionate and giving. She desperately wanted that thick, hard cock inside her, but he had purposely passed on buying condoms so he could spend the day pleasuring her.

Maybe she should be offended that he'd even had those thoughts. But she wasn't. Not even remotely so.

And as much as she wanted him to keep his promises, she was greedy, and she wanted her hands and mouth on his body. Kissing him, her tongue in his mouth, rubbing over his, was thrilling and satisfying and still not enough. With his eyes still on her, Mia broke the kiss and dotted a trail of staccato kisses down his neck. She moved her hands, tugged his shirt up, hungry to feel his skin under her hands. A flick of her tongue at the hollow of his throat confirmed her thought yesterday that he would taste like male and fresh soap and a hint of salt.

"I love that," he told her. "I love the feel of your mouth on me, and I want your mouth on my cock, but let me give you today."

"This is so insane," she mumbled.

"What?" He pushed her back gently and met her gaze. "What's insane, Mia?"

"The way I need you."

"Are you sure?"

"Yes."

Savi teased her, his tongue licking from a spot under her left ear and down to her collarbone. She breathed deeply, aroused by his scent, by his close proximity. She could feel the heat from his body on her breasts, but he stubbornly refused to touch her. His tongue bathed her skin, and then he nipped at her neck, sucking her skin into his mouth hard enough to mark her.

"Please," she whispered, and she sighed with relief when he moved. But when he only repeated the move on the right side of her neck, Mia groaned long and loud.

"What do you want?"

"Touch me."

"Where?" This time he sank his teeth into the cord of her neck hard enough to sting. But again, he rubbed the spot with his tongue and then sucked it for a moment.

"Savi." She wrapped her hands around the back of his

neck and tugged gently until his mouth hovered over her left breast. "Kiss me."

"Here?" He nuzzled her nipple with his nose.

"Yes."

Mia ducked her chin to watch him as he rubbed his lips over her breasts. His skin was warm and just a bit rough against her as he buried his face between her breasts. She breathed deeply, his fresh scent sharp and masculine. She loved his touch, his nearness, the warmth of his skin and the way his breath fanned over her each time he moved his face.

But she wanted, she needed, more.

"Savi." She combed her fingers back through his hair, a jolt of lust, emotion, shooting through her when he looked up and their eyes met. Finally, he cupped her breast in his palm and opened his mouth over her nipple. The flick of his tongue over the tight nub and the sucking motion of his lips plucked an invisible wire between her breast and her clit and chased a shiver up her spine.

Her lips moved as if in silent prayer, and she tangled her fingers in his longish, dark hair and held on. Savi suckled at her breast as if he had all the time and she were the last woman in the world. Mia held on, fingers in his hair, as he worked her sensitive skin with his teeth and his lips, over and over, until she was boneless and melting on the counter. His other hand explored her leg, starting at her ankle and tracing feather light up over her calf and her thigh.

He caught the tip of her nipple in his teeth as he flattened his palm on her thigh, and Mia's silent prayer became a chant of *yes, yes, yes*. A broken, needy sob escaped her lips when he moved his hand, up and over her shorts, his fingers on her ribs and finally, he touched her. He played with one nipple in his teeth and the other between his thumb and finger.

Ankles locked around his waist, Mia squirmed to get closer. To press her center to his erection, but Savi held her still. Just as she was ready to sob again, to beg, he switched his hand and his mouth, and suddenly his teeth worked her right nipple and his fingers pinched and tweaked the left. A long, low moan of satisfaction filled the big, open room around them. Mia's cheeks flamed when she realized the sound had come from her.

"Savi," she whispered. "I need more."

"Don't you think nipples get overlooked in foreplay?"

"What?" She let her eyelids flutter closed as he cupped both breasts in his hands now and squeezed gently. He buried his face between the curves and dragged the flat of his tongue up the valley between them.

"I think in movies, probably in real life, men go straight for that tight, wet squeeze." As he spoke, he dropped soft, sweet kisses over her breasts, pausing again to lick her nipples. "And I get that. I do. Because I can't wait to lick your clit and taste your pussy, but I'm a breast guy. And I love your nipples."

"Well, then we must be fated," she mumbled with a laugh. "Me sitting outside topless. You, a self-proclaimed breast man, showing up and finding me."

Mia felt the vibration of his laughter rumble up through his belly and his chest.

"Do you know some women can orgasm just from nipple play?"

"Is that personal experience talking? Or are you showing off with your medical knowledge of the female body?" Mia scraped her short nails up through his hair again. "Or is this knowledge something you gained from watching porn?"

He chuckled again.

"I haven't really been into porn since I had kids." He licked her, his tongue circling her nipple like the tip of an ice cream cone. "And I guess it's medical knowledge, but I can't say I read it in a textbook."

"You've never made a woman come just playing with her nipples?"

"No. But…"

"But what?" she urged him. Savi dragged his teeth over her nipple, making her shiver again.

"Well, I haven't had a quiet, cozy place with a beautiful woman like you all to myself like this since the very beginning of my marriage. No interruptions. No phone calls. No kids. And I was young in the beginning of my marriage. Probably a little greedy and a lot immature."

"And you think you can make me come playing with my nipples?"

"I love trying." He plopped a kiss between her breasts again. "Let's say that. I could lick and suck these beauties all day."

Mia swallowed hard when he turned his attention back to her right nipple and proceeded to do just that.

"Just let me…" She inched down the counter, ankles still locked at his back, and pulled him in tighter to rub her center over his hard, thick cock.

"That's cheating," he said with a laugh.

"I need it." She slipped her hand inside the collar of his shirt and spread her fingers over his back. Savi suckled her other nipple, obliging her with pressure at her center. "Savi?"

"Hmm?" He eased back a bit to trail kisses over her belly.

"This isn't it. Please tell me this isn't all we're going to do."

"This might be all we're going to do all day and night for the rest of our time here."

Mia hardly recognized the hearty laugh that slipped from her mouth.

"I need to come," she sobbed and wrapped her arms around his shoulders. "Savi. Harder. Bite me. Harder."

His teeth closed around her nipple one last time as he rocked his hard-on against her hot center and then grinded against her just enough to push her over the edge. Gentle waves of warmth washed over her. Mia dropped her head back again, arms still circling his shoulders, and let the pleasure roll through her.

"Are you okay?"

"Better than okay." She nodded. "I love your mouth."

"Yeah?"

"You're right." She loosened her legs around his waist. "Most guys give 'em a lick on the way down. To put the condom on."

She looked at Savi sheepishly, but his smile was gentle.

"Where are you going?" He touched her lips when she scooted forward. Mia glanced at the wine glasses and the cheese board. "We're not finished."

"But you made me come."

"We made you come," he said with a nod. "But that was just a warmup."

'What?"

"I wanna taste your pussy, Mia." He thumbed her nipples again.

Her mouth dry, Mia couldn't swallow. She simply stared at him, her nipples stiff peaks under his touch.

"Do you want me to kiss you there?"

"Yes."

"Are you sure?" Savi tipped his head. "It's okay if you say no."

"I want you to do everything to me," she whispered breathlessly.

Savi's eyes widened, and he flashed her a beautiful smile.

"Merry Christmas to me."

"You like this? Doing this?" She tipped her chin down to watch him unbutton and unzip her shorts.

"There's nothing I want more than to bury my face between your legs and taste you."

Mia nodded mutely as he stuck his fingers in her shorts and tugged them down. She flatted her hands on the counter to lift herself, belly free falling when he slid her shorts and panties off and dropped them to the floor.

A little uncertain now, perched nude atop the island counter, Mia nibbled at her lower lip. Savi stroked her breasts again and then gently parted her legs.

"So fucking beautiful." His awe-filled whisper made her shiver with desire. Mia gasped softly when he settled his hands on her thighs and opened her with his thumbs.

"Savi."

"Scoot back a little," he coached her.

She looked around the kitchen, noticed the tree over in the corner of the family room, and felt a ribbon of warmth curl through her belly. This was her Christmas.

This beautiful, hot man showing up and touching her and asking her if he could lick her clit to make her come. For a moment, she wondered if she was dreaming.

"Mia?" He pressed his thumb into her clit, drawing her attention away from the tree. "Are you okay?"

She grinned, the familiar rush of heat in her cheeks making her roll her eyes.

"I was just wondering if I'm dreaming."

"If you are, I am, too." His smile pulled at the ribbon in her belly. "Lay back, beautiful."

"I want to watch." The whispered words were a confession she was embarrassed to make. She tipped her chin to her chest as yet more flames touched her cheeks.

"At this angle, you'll see my tongue better if you lay back and lift your head," he told her.

"Do you do this a lot?" She giggled. "Do you perform oral sex on your nurses in supply closets?"

"I don't." He shook his head. "I promise you I don't."

Mia eased back, the granite countertop cold on her back.

Savi's hands explored her inner thighs, her belly button, and the curves of her hips. She knew better than to urge him to hurry; no man in her life had spent as much time kissing her breasts as he had. Savion did what he wanted on his own clock. He would get to her clit soon enough, and in the meantime, she would enjoy his explorations.

His fingers were soft and warm over her skin. He smoothed and traced and molded her hips and her belly and her thighs. Mia sighed with pleasure and jumped when he opened her with his thumbs again.

"Sshhh." He dropped a kiss on her hip where her panty

line would be if she weren't lying before him completely nude. "I love looking at you, Mia."

She lifted her head just enough to see him, taken aback by the heat in his dark eyes. Mia's mouth went dry when Savi licked a trail from her hip to her center, and then his eyes still locked with hers, he dipped his head and licked her seam.

"Savi," she moaned softly. He tasted her with delicate little flicks of his tongue, over her clit and her inner thighs.

"I fucking love this." His gravelly voice made her shiver.

"Don't stop."

Mia lifted herself to her elbows to watch him as he thrust his tongue inside her and then scraped his teeth over her clit. He repeated the motion, and then to Mia's delight, he spread her open and gently pushed a finger inside her.

"You're so fucking tight." He blew over her wet skin as he curled his finger inside her.

"Savi."

He added a second finger and stared at her boldly as he scissored his fingers inside her and finally curled them over a spot no other man had reached before. Mia would have doubted she had a G spot, except that she'd found it with her vibrator.

This was better, though. Savi's eyes glazed with lust roaming up and down her body. His body heat heavy between her legs. His fingers moving inside her. His open mouth over her, his tongue rubbing over her clit, and then his teeth working the small nub before he sucked her into his mouth.

Mia's arms quivered as she fought to watch him. Intense waves of heat and pleasure rolled over her. Savi lifted his head to look at her again, still sliding and plunging his fingers inside her. Mia lifted one hand to stroke her own breast, the thrill on Savi's face pushing her to tweak her nipple.

"Savi," she whispered.

"Come for me, Mia." He kissed a trail down her left thigh and then nipped his way back up to her clit, all the while using his fingers to make her crazy. "I've got you. Let go, come for me."

Mia moaned loudly as she lowered herself back to the counter. Her arms still quivered, and she still touched herself, desperately chasing the languid, delicious pleasure Savi had promised.

"I'm so close." She stared blindly at the ceiling and used her heels to push her hips from the counter to grind against Savi's face.

"You taste like sex, Mia." He drew circles over her clit with the tip of his tongue. "Like summer and the ocean and sweat and cum and woman. I love you on my mouth."

"Savi." She lifted her right hand and tangled her fingers in his hair to press his face closer. Savi sucked her sensitive nub into his mouth again and plunged his fingers one last time as Mia's body seized on the counter, and she cried his name out on a harsh sob.

"Jesus, that was perfect." He dropped a sweet kiss low on her belly as he inched his way up her body.

Mia laughed softy and wiped at her eyes.

"That's my line, Savion." Her voice shook with emotion, with the aftereffects of the orgasm that left her quivering with delight.

"I think you're the most beautiful woman I've ever seen."

He kissed a line up between her breasts and then nuzzled her with his nose. Mia gasped when he flicked her nipple with his tongue again.

"No." She laughed and caught his head between her hands. "Too much. It's too much. I need a minute."

"Can you sit up?"

"Yeah."

Savi took her hands in his and helped her sit up on the counter.

"Taste this, Mia," he whispered, lowering his mouth to hers. "This drives me fucking crazy, tasting you on my tongue."

Mia hesitated, kissing him with only her lips, but Savi drew her in with his arms around her back and his tongue gently sliding between her lips. She tasted herself, her arousal, on his lips and his tongue, shocked to feel that need building inside her again already.

"That's never happened before." She rested her forehead on his shoulder.

"An orgasm like that?"

"I can come with my fingers or my vibrator. But I rarely come during sex, and I've never come like that."

"With someone licking you?"

She nodded.

"Did you like it?"

"Did I like it?" she whispered with a laugh. "Can I take you home with me? You're so much better than the vibrator."

Savi's happy laugh filled the room.

"You're a beautiful man." She lifted her head to meet his eyes. "And you're really good at that."

"Only as good as the woman I'm with." He kissed the tip of her nose.

"I love the way you talk dirty, too."

"Do you want that wine now?"

"Sure." She offered him a dreamy smile.

"Do you wanna go back outside?"

"I wanna lay with you," she told him. "In your bed. Naked. And drink wine. And touch you. And kiss you."

CHAPTER 9

SAVI

"That sounds pretty perfect."

Savi held her hands when Mia inched forward, and then he palmed her hips and lifted her from the counter.

"You're way overdressed." She nipped at his earlobe and then ducked her head to sink her teeth into the curve between his shoulder and neck.

"You feel good against me." Savi tipped his head back and caught her mouth in a hungry kiss. "Grab the wine."

"What about the cheese?"

"I'll come back for it," he promised. "I'm gonna need a little sustenance."

"Like cheese is gonna fill you up." She laughed and grabbed the wineglasses when Savi carried her closer to them.

"Have you talked to Lane?" she asked as Savi walked her across the open living area to the casita door. "Let me down."

Mia dragged her legs slowly over his hips and his

outer thighs as she lowered them to stand. Savi's cock strained at his zipper, hungry for the feel of her pressed against him again.

"I talked to Lane for a second yesterday."

"Are you gonna tell him about this?"

"I don't kiss and tell." Savi wrapped his hand around the back of her neck and pulled her close for another hungry, wet kiss. "Are you gonna tell Toni?"

Mia's lips curved under his.

"I don't wanna kiss and tell, either, but I do." She pressed her breasts to his chest again. "We need to get horizontal, Savi."

"You don't want to, but you do?"

"How do you expect me to keep my mouth shut about that orgasm? Delivered by your incredible mouth? Looking into your eyes when you went down on me? Girls have to share those secrets with someone."

Savi chuckled and shook his head. He stepped back for a moment, opened the door, and followed Mia inside. He had no idea if she'd been inside the casita before, but since there was only one bedroom, she couldn't miss it. Savi pulled the covers back as Mia put the glasses on the nightstand.

"You make your bed on vacation?"

He grinned and shrugged. "Maybe I was hoping to get you in here and impress you."

"Oh, you're gonna impress me." She nodded. "And that's nothing to do with your made bed."

"I'll be right back," he promised as he took a step backwards.

"'kay. I'll be waiting."

He froze in the doorway when Mia stretched out over

the bed sideways. She lay on her belly, propped on her elbows, and turned to look at him.

"I can't walk away when you look that damned sexy."

"Sorry." She turned over to her back and lifted her arms over her head.

"Yeah, not helping." He shook his head. "Don't move."

"Nowhere else I want to be."

Her words wrapped around his shoulders as he hurried back out to the main kitchen. He considered cleaning the counter, thought of Mia naked and waiting for him, and decided it could wait. Feeling like a real hero, Savi picked up the cheese board and carried it back to the casita. Everything else could wait. He had a woman to please.

He wondered if Mia would want to continue this after Christmas. If she would want to see him again. He damned sure wanted to see her again, to hear her laugh, to see that cute little blush, to taste her pussy, and fuck yes, he wanted to take her to bed night after night. Might be difficult to carry on a long-distance relationship, but he was willing.

Then again, if this was just a fun Christmas fling for her, he wouldn't push it. Would he? He didn't want to make her uncomfortable. And he wasn't the clingy, stalking type. But damned if he wasn't falling fast for Mia.

"You were gone way too long."

Savi stopped in his tracks at the sight of her. Mia had moved to put her head on a pillow. She lay on her back, legs parted and knees bent. Which gave Savi a front row view of her pussy. His cock throbbed again and strained against his zipper.

"Were you thinking about touching yourself?" he asked hopefully.

"I could." She lifted a shoulder, the sound of her body moving on the steel gray sheets sexy as fuck. "But I'd rather touch you."

"I told you today is about you."

"Well, I want to touch you." She sat up to reach for him. "And you have to give me what I want, right?"

"Mmm." He groaned. "You're hard to say no to."

"Good." She shrugged. "That's settled. I wanna see you naked, Savion Merchant."

Savi walked farther into the room and put the cheese board by the glasses. Mia watched him with hooded eyes as he tugged his shirt up and over his head.

"Jesus." She sighed, eyes dipping from his shoulders to the trail of hair that led to his cock, bursting at the fly of his shorts. "Perfection."

"Hardly."

"I wanna bite you," she announced.

"Yeah?" He grinned and tossed his shirt on the bed. When she grabbed it and held it to her nose to sniff it, every ounce of blood in Savi's body pulsed in his cock.

"You smell yummy." She turned her attention back to him. "C'mere."

Savi eased his knee onto the bed, floored when Mia reached and threw her arm around his shoulder. The skin to skin contact was sensory overload for him. He jumped and groaned when she sank her teeth into his upper arm and then sucked hard enough to bruise him.

He hissed and clenched his teeth.

"You're gonna make me come in my shorts."

"Take 'em off," she suggested. "Then you can come

on me."

"Fuck." Savi's hands trembled as he struggled with his button and zipper. Mia distracted him with soft, sweet kisses over his neck. Finally, he kicked out of the shorts, only to have Mia cup his length in her hand.

"You don't have *just one condom*?" she whispered.

"I want you to enjoy this."

"I never said I didn't enjoy sex," she answered. "Just that I don't orgasm often."

"Well, I wanna give you a record number of orgasms."

"Okay, but I like sex, Savi. And I like being this close to you."

She raked her fingers up through the back of his hair and pressed her open mouth to his for a long, wet kiss.

"Let me kiss you again." He eased her back to the mattress, but Mia surprised him and flipped him over to straddle him.

"Please tell me you have at least one condom." She flicked her tongue over his nipple. "Don't guys carry condoms in their wallets? Isn't that a thing? A guy rule?"

He laughed and lifted his arms to wrap them around her.

"I have a couple in my wallet."

"Thank fuck," she muttered as she backed over him and dragged her tongue down his belly.

"If you put your mouth on me now, I'll come," he warned her. "I dreamt about this last night, after seeing you topless out by the pool. I've wanted to do this since the second I saw you—"

Mia opened her mouth over his cock, her breath hot through his boxer briefs.

"Wallet." He could barely grind the word out.

"Where is it?"

"The drawer of the nightstand."

She stretched sideways, her breast grazing his hip, and pulled the drawer open. Savi smoothed his hands over her ass cheeks as she retrieved his wallet.

"Are they in there?"

He sure as fuck hoped so. If he was mistaken after Mia had all but begged him to fuck her, his cock might actually break.

"You want my fingers in your wallet?"

"Nothing to hide, Mia."

Their eyes locked, and she hesitated for a second, finally breaking the eye contact and opening his wallet, wailing with relief when she plucked two condoms out.

"Hurry," she urged him.

"I don't wanna hurry this."

"Savi, fuck me." She wiggled over his cock, leaving his briefs wet. "Next time, we can make it slow and sweet and tender and all that good stuff. But right now, I need this inside me. I need it hard and fast. I want—"

Savi flipped her, stealing a kiss as he did so. Her choppy breaths sent his heartrate hammering hard and fast. With her eyes on him, he shimmied backwards off the bed and tugged his briefs down to kick out of them.

"Oh, God." Mia sighed, eyes wide with hunger. "Yes. Give it to me, Savi."

He tore the wrapper open and rolled the condom on as Mia sat up again and reached for him. She dug her fingers into his hips and dragged him forward, falling to lay on the bed beneath him. Long hair spread over the pillows, the swollen-kissed-the-fuck-out-of-me lips parted, eyes wide with wonder, she looked like an angel.

Savi's angel.

God help him, he never wanted to let her go.

"Mia."

"Yes."

He eased into her slowly, inch by inch. Their eyes locked as he filled her, Mia tilting her hips to take him deep. When his balls were pressed hot and tight against her, they plunged together for another wild kiss, teeth knocking and lips stinging. Savi filled his hands with her hot, sticky skin. He thumbed her nipples and then pinched them hard as he pumped his hips hard and fast against her.

Mia moved with him, thrust for thrust, feet planted on the bed, hips in the air under him. Her hands roamed his back, squeezing his ass cheeks and then scraping a trail up his back as he moved inside her.

"I want you to come," he told her. "That pussy is so fucking delicious, but I want you to feel good, too."

"Come, Savi." She bit his chin and then sucked his lower lip into her mouth, still moving with him.

"Touch yourself," he told her.

"I wanna touch you."

As if to reiterate her point, she dragged her hands down his back and reached between their bodies to touch his balls. Savi felt a tingle in his lower back, the tension already building.

"Touch yourself while I'm inside you," he insisted. "Please, Mia. Rub your clit."

He slowed for a moment and looked at the spot where their bodies were joined.

"Bend your knees and touch yourself."

She did as he told her, his cock still buried deep inside

her. He moved slowly, deliberately, and watched her fingers slide over her clit.

"Does it feel good?" he asked her.

"Feels so fucking good," she moaned. "But I won't—"

"Let it feel good, Mia." His voice was gruff with his need to control himself. "Am I at a good angle? Do I feel good inside you?"

She laughed softly, her grin tugging at his heartstrings.

"You feel incredible, Savi."

"Okay. Let me be your sex toy. You do whatever you need to do to get off."

"Does this turn you on?"

"You have no fucking idea how hot you are right now," he promised her. Mia lifted her head again to look at him.

He thought she was going to argue, but she tilted her hips a bit more, bit her lower lip, and rubbed her clit in small circular motions. Savi moved inside her, his eyes glued to the spot where their bodies were joined.

"Feels good." She tipped her chin up; the words slipping out of her mouth on a soft gasp.

"Don't hold back." Savi smoothed his hands over her thighs and cupped her ass cheeks, straining to go deeper, to find the spot to drive Mia wild.

Mia's eyelids fluttered as she quickened the pace of her fingers and found her breast with her free hand. Lips parted, she panted and moaned and chanted his name. Savi grit his teeth and slowed the rock of his hips for her pleasure and for his control. The way she cried out, her voice full of wonder and surrender, when she came, made his chest ache.

"Oh my God."

Savi watched her body quiver with aftershocks, her

fingers clamped tight around her nipple and her other hand sliding loosely now over her clit. She lifted her hips from the bed again, her thighs tightening against him. He wondered if her toes were curled.

"Savi." She licked her lips. When she opened her eyes, the glaze of lust and pleasure in them drove him to lean over her and steal a long, tender kiss.

"That was the hottest thing I've ever seen," he told her.

"Don't hold back." She turned his words around on him, wrapping her legs around his waist when he rode her harder, faster. Her feet at his ass spurred him on, and he had a quick fantasy of fucking her in stilettos. Maybe they could try that, too. A fancy dinner, some dancing, and some kinky sex with heels and her wrists bound in his tie.

Mia squeezed against him, her pussy wet and tight around his cock. Hands on his back, her fingernails scraping his skin with need and satisfaction, the image of her in nothing but stiletto heels and his black and red tie, Savi bucked against her one last time. His body tightened with his release, and he dropped his head to her shoulder where he pressed his lips to her skin to ride out the orgasm.

Several moments passed, their choppy, gasping breaths the only sound in the room. Mia kept her legs around his waist; he could still feel her tightening around his cock to draw his pleasure out. Finally, aware that he was much heavier than she was, Savi rolled off of her and gathered her to lie pressed to his side.

She cut loose with a long, deep moan of contentment and curled into him, her face resting on his chest, her hand on his belly.

"I don't ever want to move," she whispered.

"Well, as soon as that second condom's used, we're gonna have to move."

Her soft laugh fanned over his chest.

"As much as I love you right now, I kinda wanna kick you." Mia pressed her lips to his chest and rubbed her hand up over his belly to touch his nipple. Savi's heart hitched just under her face. She used the word *love*. Obviously, she was referring to the sex, to the orgasm that looked fan-fucking-tastic to him, but for a second, he wanted it to mean more.

"Why do you wanna kick me?" He played with her hair and turned his head to look at her when she tipped her chin up.

"I can't believe you were thinking about this in the grocery store, and you didn't buy condoms."

"I know." He nodded. "But I had good intentions," he reminded her. "I would have been happy with my face between your legs for the rest of the day. I don't think I'll ever get enough of you. Of the way you taste."

"I don't think I'll ever get enough of you."

Savi grinned when she moved her hand to cup his cock.

"Wow." She stretched up to nibble his chin as his cock sprang to life in her fingers.

Hungry again for her kiss, Savi cupped her chin in his hand as she stretched toward him again. This kiss was slow, tender, all the things that Savi knew it was too soon to say, to feel, wrapped up in the way his mouth, his tongue moved in hers.

"After we get more condoms," she whispered, "I'd be good with never leaving your bed."

CHAPTER 10

MIA

They left the bedroom to get condoms later that night. Mia floated through the aisles behind Savi, feeling like a lovesick teen, hanging onto his hand and dying to finish their purchase and take things back to the casita where they could be alone.

But when he suggested ice cream on the way back, the idea surprised her and delighted her so much, she laughed and said yes, so instead of rushing back to bed to go another round, they sat outside and licked ice cream cones. The sweet, cold treat was delicious, and after spending the afternoon in bed with him, Mia's thoughts went straight to licking the ice cream from Savi's body. Judging from the look in Savi's eyes, he was entertaining the same thoughts about her.

It was fun, but Mia decided, also dangerous. She had just met Savi, and already she was attached. Those feelings might have been easier for her to swallow, to shrug away, if she could write it off as sexual satisfaction. After all, there were only one or two times she remembered reaching orgasm with a partner before him, and those experiences had been less than earth-shattering compared to the way Savion had wrecked her.

But eating ice cream and feeling the cool evening air on her arms and listening to Savi tell her about a Christmas when he was up until four in the morning assembling toys for the kids? Laughing when he said he was so tired, he poured orange juice in his coffee rather than milk that Christmas morning, their fingers intertwined on the bench between them.

She wanted more sex with him. She had six more days in Arizona before she had to go home. Mia wanted nothing more than to spend those six days nude, playing, making love with Savi. But hanging out like this, hanging out by the pool last night after dinner, made her want more.

Odds were, Savi wouldn't be interested in anything more than a fun vacation romp. He had a life in Milwaukee. He was a doctor, for God's sake. He wouldn't leave his practice for her. And even if by some miracle he did, he had children who lived in Milwaukee. Mia didn't feel that his ex-wife was a threat, but she would never attempt to take him from his kids.

"What're you thinking?" he asked as they walked hand in hand to his rented Range Rover.

Busted with thoughts about feelings, she blushed and shook her head.

"You can't possibly blush anymore," he reminded her. "I am intimately acquainted with every inch of your body. And I love it. From your head to your toes."

She laughed softly. Savi opened her door for her, but

he wrapped his fingers around her upper arm and dropped a kiss on her cheek.

"I love the way you love it," she answered, hoping to distract him.

"What're you thinking?" He brushed his lips over the corner of her mouth. "Tell me."

"Just..." She swallowed hard and shook her head. "Things better left unsaid."

"Regrets?"

"No."

He studied her face for a moment and finally nodded. The drive back to the casita was comfortably quiet, and once there, they crawled into bed together, fully clothed, and napped. Mia awoke sometime later to Savi's fingers stroking her breast and his lips on the back of her neck. Without a word, she turned in his arms to start again.

THEY DID LEAVE HIS BED AGAIN, THOUGH THEY SPENT THE nights there together. Mia was thrilled with his suggestions for dates. She hesitated to think of their time that way, but when a man wined you and dined you—insisted you wear the one cocktail dress you packed with the red heels you packed even if you doubted you would need them—and then brought you back to a private place to dance with you and strip you down to nothing but the heels to make love to you, what else did you call it?

Mornings they spent by the pool with coffee and books and then they made breakfast together. The day before his ex-wife's wedding, they hiked Cholla Trailhead on Camelback Mountain. Mia had been right about Savi being in excellent shape. The first part of the trail was easier, just trail hiking, though Mia was constantly on the lookout for rattlesnakes. But once they got to the saddle, the hike was more intense. So intense, Mia had to stop sneaking peeks at the hard muscles in Savi's calves, imagining running her tongue up over them to tickle the backs of his knees and further up, to sink her teeth into his perfect ass cheeks. She paid more attention to the loose gravel and the worry about wildlife, as well as having to dig deep to find the stamina to keep going.

That evening, after a shower, they sat together in the hot tub. Between the sex marathon—a completely new experience for Mia—and the hike—something she did, but not often—her body hurt everywhere, and kicking back in the hot tub to stargaze with Savi was perfect. He suggested another hot tub visit the next night, as they had an afternoon trip to Topgolf planned, which would involve swinging a golf club repeatedly and eventually make them sore on top of the already sore muscles from the hike. Half asleep, head tipped back, Savi's hard body at her side, Mia mumbled that as long as she was with him, she would be happy.

She was so far gone, so into him, she didn't question what she'd said or attempt to take it back.

Savi didn't panic. In fact, he moved closer to her and brushed a chaste kiss over her shoulder.

After a long soak, they climbed from the hot tub, wrapped up in towels, and went inside to dress. Mia pulled on red silk panties and Savi's T-shirt that hung just over her butt. Savi eyed her with a greedy smile, which made her think of the night they'd done dinner and then dancing back here in the living room. After he made love to her in nothing but her heels, he'd slipped his tie around her neck and knotted it loosely.

She had let him take a picture of her. In the tie and the heels. And the glow of sexual satisfaction. Maybe she should have said no, maybe she should worry about him carrying a nude photo of her on his phone. She didn't. As his eyes heated when he watched her pull his T-shirt on now, she decided she would have posed for a hundred more.

Just for him.

They'd had homemade pizza the night they'd gone back to the store to get condoms. Mia would never have suspected homemade pizza at midnight could be such a turn on. But it was. Their dinner out was seafood and wine, and the song they danced to when they came back to the casita and Savi turned on his phone—only one, because they couldn't keep their hands off each other— was "When A Man Loves A Woman" and as they danced, Savi sang along with Percy Sledge.

Which, Mia had to remind herself, meant nothing. A lot of people sang or hummed along with songs. It wasn't his way of saying he was falling in love with her. Or maybe it was a nod to the fact that they'd shared a special time together, but it didn't mean anything once the holidays were over.

"We could grill something," he suggested now.

Mia leaned on the island, the opposite end from where he had first wrecked her with his mouth just a few days ago, and watched him peruse the refrigerator and then the freezer.

"We could."

She didn't want to grill. Though she was hungry, the hike had exhausted her. They had already decided to go out for Mexican food tomorrow after they left Topgolf, and they had tentatively discussed what they would eat together for Christmas dinner. Mia had offered to fix noodles and dressing, and Savi would roast a turkey breast.

"Sub sandwiches?" He looked at her over his shoulder and arched his eyebrows.

"Perfect," she agreed. "Minimal effort required is perfect. My body still hurts."

Savi started pulling deli meats and cheeses from the fridge. He shot her a quick glance.

"We don't have to make love every night," he reminded her. "It's okay. I love having you in my bed. Sleeping with you in my arms."

She grinned as she rounded the counter and went to the pantry to find bread.

"I love sleeping in your arms," she told him. She plucked a loaf of French bread from the shelf, grabbed a bag of chips, and returned to the island to stand by him. "But do you know how I would feel if I went home in a few days and didn't take advantage of every chance I had to be with you that way?"

Her heart pushed up into her throat, making it difficult to swallow. This was as close as she had come to really admitting her feelings for him. She was terrified of how he would react. Mia had never believed in insta-love, and granted, there was a lot they had to learn about each other. But she had no desire to just flip the switch and put the fire out when it was time to go home. There was something real between them, a connection she hadn't felt before, and she wanted desperately for him to feel the same way.

What if he scoffed at the idea? What if he was just an incredibly good lover who took the time to treasure the women he was with?

Their eyes locked; Savi still hadn't responded. Mia took a quick breath and turned to move away.

"Mia." His voice the same low, gruff tone he used when he was inside her, Mia nearly came undone at the counter. Again. She held her breath and looked back at him. "I feel the same way."

She sighed, relieved, but still uncertain. Because he could mean that he didn't want to miss any opportunity to fuck her. To enjoy her body. Or he could have read her heart, her soul, in her eyes, and maybe he did feel the same way she did.

She nodded, mostly so she could step away from the intense moment. The intimacy in the eye contact at this moment was so much deeper, so raw, even compared to the times they were together in his bed, that she couldn't breathe. Or think.

"Mia?" Savi reached for her hand when she took the twist tie off the bread.

"What do you think? A beer tonight? With sandwiches?"

Savi stepped closer to her, cupped her chin, and turned her to face him.

"What do you think?"

His thumb traced softly over her lips, his eyes lowering to study her mouth before meeting her gaze again.

"When the holidays are over?"

She swallowed hard, afraid to answer him.

"Would you wanna see me again?"

"Yes."

That question was easy to answer. She almost crossed her fingers in hopes that he felt the same way, but she caught herself. Wishes and finger crosses were for kids. She and Savi were adults with their own lives, and they would need more than that to find a way to be together.

"Yes?" His lips tipped up in a sloppy, happy grin. "Like...in a-let's-meet-back-here-next-year-for-a-Christmas-visit thing? Or in a...you-would-come-to-Milwaukee-to-see-me...like...next month way?"

Mia nibbled on her lip and chuckled. "I'd love to spend every—I'd love to spend the holidays with you next year like this." She covered his hand with hers and brought his fingers to her mouth to kiss them. "And I'd love to visit you in Milwaukee next month."

"Even if there was snow?"

"Even if."

"And if I had my kids or had to pick them up or run them to a practice or help with homework?"

"I'd love to meet your kids, Savi, but if you think that's moving too fast, I would understand that. I get it. You're a dad. You're involved in your kids' lives." She leaned in to kiss him. "I like that about you."

"Would you ever invite me to visit you?"

"I would." She nodded.

"Did we just agree to maybe do a long-distance...relationship?"

"Can I ask you one thing?"

"Of course."

She nodded, but she hesitated. She would commit to a

long-distance thing with him. In a heartbeat. If they got closer, if things continued as they were and they got serious, she would consider moving to be with him. But eventually she would need more.

How could she ask a man she'd only known for a few days if he wanted more children?

"What is it?" Savi put his arm around her and drew her close. "Mia, talk to me."

"I want...I want to see you again. I can't imagine this being over in just a few more days. But..." She licked her lips. "You have kids. And I'm sure I would love your kids." She smiled sadly. "What about the future? I'm not asking you to commit to me, but what if things get serious, and you don't want more children?"

Savi brushed his lips over her forehead.

"I promise you that if things get serious, I would be all in. Marriage. My kids. Babies with you. Sharing a house. Sharing our lives."

Mia puffed her cheeks up and arched her eyebrows.

"You okay?" he asked with a frown.

"Terrified," she answered with a laugh. "More so now than the moment I realized you were spying on me that first day you walked in and saw me topless by the pool."

"You were scared of me then?"

"I didn't know you," she reminded him. "You could have been a burglar or a murderer."

"And you're more afraid of me now than when you thought I might be here to do you harm?"

Mia shook her head slowly and wrapped her arms around his shoulders.

"I'm scared of me. Of you. Of how big, how full, you make my heart. It's so fast, I'm scared of it."

"Do you like roller coasters?" He dropped a peck on her lips.

"I do."

"Okay. Well. Let's enjoy this ride together. See where it goes."

"Roller coasters take you right back where you started."

"Mmm." Savi nodded and looked over her shoulder at the island. "I seem to remember starting right here. With my mouth on you."

"You're incorrigible!" She ducked her chin and rested her forehead on his shoulder.

"How about you grab us a couple of beers, and I'll slap these sandwiches together?"

"Okay."

Mia went to the fridge for the longnecks and looked over her shoulder at the man who had turned her world upside down in just a few short days. He made her weak in the knees, and he made her heart happy, and he made her want everything in the world a man could give a woman.

She had just committed to starting something, to continuing something with him. Only time would tell how things would work out.

CHAPTER 11

SAVI

He wouldn't have given Blair's wedding any thought at all, if Mia hadn't asked about the kids, about how they dealt with his divorce and how they got along with Micah and if Savi's visitation schedule would change much after the wedding. Not that he thought he would be wallowing away the night before his ex-wife's second wedding.

But still. There had been a time when Savi was completely wrapped up in Blair, and she was crazy about him. They had some good memories, and of course, they had created two incredible children together, so he would never look at his first marriage as a waste of time. He wasn't necessarily pining over Blair, over the fact that she was getting remarried. But he had come to Arizona to get away from the idea of it. To hold those memories at bay and keep his mind on other things.

And Mia had certainly kept his mind on other things.

He hadn't expected to come to Arizona and find someone new, either. Not even for a hook up. Savi had simply wanted some time to relax. When things had gone sideways between himself and Blair, he really didn't expect to find someone else. He had always been too busy, too focused on work, on his patients, which had been part of the problem between them.

But now here he was falling for a woman he'd just met a few days ago, so completely into her, it didn't bother him at all to tell Mia both Aszia and Drew would be in the wedding party, as small as it was. He had no idea who else was involved, how many guests Blair and Micah had invited. He didn't care. But he cared about his kids, and he was relieved they were happy to be included. Blair had even sent him photos of the kids when they had gone dress shopping and when Drew was fitted for a new suit. Savi was always a proud father, but he was especially proud that his children had bounced back from the divorce and were able to accept Blair's new love into their lives.

Which made him hopeful that if things progressed with Mia as he hoped they would, they would accept her, too.

When he boarded his flight to come here, he figured he would catch up on his reading or watch a movie the night before Blair's wedding. The day of the wedding. On his ex's second wedding night. And now, here he was curled up on the casita sofa with a beautiful woman, watching Christmas movies.

Hallmark Christmas movies.

And even better? He was enjoying himself. It was obvious to him that Mia loved the overly sweet, terribly predictable movies, even if she did roll her eyes and laugh at some of the cheesy scenes. Savi popped popcorn between movies, and they snacked on it together. In the past, he would have been ready to cry uncle after two, but snuggled up with Mia, he was content to stay on the sofa with her all evening.

They turned the TV off before midnight and shared the bathroom space as they got ready for bed. Savi didn't watch Mia and compare her to Blair. He simply watched her and wondered where she had been all of his life.

On the second night they spent together, Mia had told him she found a stack of 80s movies in the guest suite, so they raided that closet together and watched *Sixteen Candles*. The next night they watched *The Outsiders*. When Mia confessed to having a thing for Matt Dillon, Savi teased her and threatened to turn the movie off. The end result was a wrestling match in bed, which resulted in Mia going down on him and taking him in her mouth. After she'd brought him to orgasm, he went to sleep with her in his arms, not terribly worried about Matt Dillon.

Tonight, they went to bed in the dark and turned to each other without hesitation. Sex between them had been everything from sensual to hard core and dirty, and Mia seemed to like all of it just as much as Savi did. But he chose to love her slowly this time, with tender strokes and kisses that Mia returned without hesitation.

A buzzing sound woke him what felt like only minutes later. Mia stirred when Savi flipped over to his back, but she only turned over to lay on her side. Sunlight beat at the closed shutters over the window, but he couldn't guess what time it was. He knew it was his ex-wife's wedding day, but Savi's only plans for the day were to be at Mia's side, doing anything and everything that would make her happy. Topgolf. Mexican food. A whole lot of kissing and touching.

Identifying the noise finally, he stretched to grab his phone. Blair's name and number flashed on the screen. Seemed a bit odd for her to call him on her wedding day. Savi knew damned well she didn't have cold feet. For one thing, his ex had balls of steel, and she was a woman, so that was saying something. And another, Savi knew her well enough to know she was very much in love with Micah, that they would be happy together.

Which meant Blair calling him now was bad. Something was wrong.

He tapped accept, sat up, and swung his legs around the edge of the bed as he said hello. Mia mumbled something in her sleep. Savi felt a pang of fear in his chest. Worry for Blair. For his kids. For what this phone call was going to mean to Mia.

"Dad?"

Savi was shocked to hear his son's voice on the line instead of Blair's.

"Hey, Drew." He climbed out of bed and glanced back at Mia. Still sleeping. So peaceful. She was nude, but wrapped in the sheet and blanket, so Savi could only see her neck and shoulders and the slope of her back. Not wanting to wake her, he slipped out of the bedroom and gently pulled the door closed behind him. He padded out to the casita kitchen and looked at the microwave clock. Just after eight. Which made it after eleven there. The wedding would be later this evening.

"Aszia is hurt."

"What?" Savi fought to remain calm. Aszia being hurt could be something as simple as a stubbed toe. How many times had he and Blair told her she could win an Oscar with some of her dramatic performances? But it could also mean something terrible. She had a driver's permit, so Savi's mind wanted to jump the car-accident train. Or maybe she'd fallen down the steps at his in-laws' house. Or—

"We're in the ER," Drew told him.

Savi flinched. He ducked his head and scrubbed his free hand back through his hair.

"What happened?" Savi willed his heart to slow down. Nothing good would come of him having a panic attack on top of whatever happened to Aszia.

"We were sledding."

"This morning?"

"Yeah."

"Were Mom and Micah out, too?"

That seemed odd to Savi, but then, maybe if he and Mia were bunked up somewhere with snow with his kids, they would head out to go sled riding the morning of their wedding, too. Savi had no doubt Blair and Micah enjoyed doing the things he and Mia had been doing for the past few days, but he also had no doubt that he and Mia would have fun with his kids if their places were reversed right now.

"Yeah." Drew sounded five again, instead of eleven.

"Drew, bud, where's Mom? Can I talk to her?"

"She's with Aszia in the exam room."

"Okay, what about Micah?"

"He's at the nurse thing, the desk. Talking to them. I rode with him. Mom came in the ambulance with Aszia."

Ambulance?

Savi felt his knees go weak.

"Drew. What happened? What's wrong with Aszia?"

He pictured his little girl in a heap of broken bones at the bottom of a hill. Or what if she'd hit a tree? Or if a low-hanging branch had caught her and cut her? Savi knew someone who had his throat cut when he was a kid. His sled went AWOL, and the kid got hung up on a branch.

"She was crying," Drew announced. "So was Mom."

Savi gritted his teeth together and sighed. He needed more information. Drew was old enough to communicate exact details, but he was also close to his sister, and obviously shaken by the accident. Savi had no way of knowing how badly Aszia was injured.

"Hey."

He looked up to find Mia at the counter watching him with concern.

"Drew. What about now? Can I talk to Micah now?"

"Still talking to a nurse."

"Do they know you have Mom's phone?"

"I don't know. Micah has her purse, so I took it. If I were Aszia, I would want you to be here."

"Oh, Drew." Savi squeezed his eyes closed, his son's words an arrow in his heart. Of course, he needed to be there. No matter what was going on, he had to change his flight and get to his daughter as soon as possible. He had always been that dad, the one who was there for both kids. As much as he hated to leave Mia, he had to go.

"Her leg looked really gross, Dad," Drew told him.

"Gross? Like she cut it?"

"No, like a bone was totally sticking out of it," Drew answered.

Savi muttered curse words his son didn't often hear him say.

"Okay. Will you please have Mom or Micah call me? As soon as they know something? I'm gonna start packing, okay, Drew? Can you do that?"

"I will."

"Okay. Love you, bud."

"Love you, too, Dad."

Savi huffed with frustration when he set his phone down on the counter. Mia, dressed in one of his T-shirts and nothing else, leaned forward to rest her elbows on the counter.

"What happened?"

"Sled riding accident," he mumbled. "All I know is they took Aszia to the hospital by ambulance. Something about a bone sticking out of her leg."

"Oh." Mia cringed. "Sounds like a compound fracture."

"It does," he agreed. He dipped his head and pinched his nose. "I'm not sure. I don't know if she's hurt so badly, she needs me. Drew seemed to think she does."

"Savi—"

"Or if it's that Drew is scared and needs me there."

Mia nodded, her face drawn and sad, and stepped around the counter.

"Either way, you should go," she said quietly.

"I hate this, Mia." He straightened and stepped toward her to take her in his arms. "I hate leaving you at all, and I really hate running out on you like this."

"It's okay."

"We had Christmas plans."

"It's just food," she reminded him.

"Oh, no. I was gonna lay you down by the tree and make love to you."

"Mmm." She arched her eyebrows and offered him a small smile. "I would have liked that."

"I could wait. See if Blair calls back."

Mia shook her head. "Go shower. I'll make you some coffee."

CHAPTER 12

MIA

She hated that he had to leave, but what choice did he have? She knew in just the short amount of time she had known him that Savi was a good father. He wouldn't feel right abandoning either child now, whether Aszia was that badly injured or if it was just that Drew was shaken up and wanted him around. And Mia had to let him go. Maybe it was a gamble, but it was one she had to take for him.

Still in Savi's T-shirt, because she planned to keep it forever even if she didn't get to keep Savi forever, she slipped her panties on and went to the main kitchen to make coffee. She could have used the coffee maker in the casita, but if she had to say goodbye to him, the casita was too cozy, too much of them together there. She didn't want to risk getting emotional when he left. Mia didn't want to make him feel guilty for doing what he had to do. What he wanted to do.

Once the coffee was going, she stood in the open door

of the fridge, looking for something quick she could fix him for breakfast. She decided on a smoothie, so he could take it with him. Who knew what the airport was going to look like, whether it would be nuts right before Christmas or dead because people were already home for the holidays. Anything she could do to save him some time would be good.

She glanced at the tree in the corner of the room as she splashed juice into the blender. No matter that he had to leave so soon, so suddenly, this would be a cherished holiday memory. It was too soon. She knew it. She knew her friends and family would warn her. But she was falling for Savion Merchant, and she was scared that this sudden plot twist would come between them. Not because she doubted his feelings, but because they were so new, their relationship so new and fragile, real life could come charging in and consume them, and if too much time passed, maybe neither of them would be inclined to travel, to put effort into a relationship that spanned so many miles.

Mia added blueberries and a banana to the blender, eyes still roaming to the tree every few minutes. The last few days had been packed with so much fun, so much intimacy. From their outings—hiking and the fancy dinner to name a couple—to the moments they'd spent here alone, Mia had loved every moment. She'd had more sex in the past few days than ever in her life, and Savi had done something special for her. She'd never before made love. She wasn't sure she would ever know the difference, but now she did. Being with Savi was different.

And damned if she didn't regret that he wasn't going

to be able to lay her down by the tree and make love to her on Christmas.

The sound of the casita door closing drew her attention from the blender, her mind from Savi's Christmas plans. Mia felt her heart drop when she saw him standing there with his luggage.

This was really happening.

Only time would tell, she reminded herself. They had exchanged numbers and addresses, so she had to hope that he would contact her. Let her know how Aszia was doing. And hopefully ask to see her soon.

"I made you some coffee," she told him. "And a smoothie. For breakfast. I know you have to be hungry, but I know you need to get going."

Savi nodded and ambled over to the counter. He took the travel mug she'd filled for him, eyes on the Tervis cup with the smoothie. She wondered if Lane and Toni would notice the cups were missing. She wondered what Toni would say if she knew Mia had come out here to relax and lost her heart to this man.

"I'm sorry."

"It's okay." Mia shook her head. She stepped closer and touched his lips with her finger. "I hate that you have to go, but I get it."

Savi nodded again, but he was quiet.

"Has Blair called? Do you know what's going on yet?"

"No. And I called her twice. I keep getting her voicemail. I got Micah's voicemail."

"Okay." Mia leaned in closer to kiss him. Just a soft brush of her lips over his. "Keep trying. I know your mind is racing right now."

"It can't be life threatening," he mumbled. "Blair would have called me herself if Aszia was critically injured."

"I know," Mia agreed. She patted his chest. "I know. But I know you need to be there. To see your little girl for yourself. To make sure she's okay."

Savi tipped his chin up and studied Mia's face with an intensity that made her heart hurt.

"And I know you need to be there with Drew, while Aszia's being treated."

"I feel like an ass leaving you like this."

"Savi." Mia shook her head. "This is the man I'm falling for. The one who loves his kids and cares enough to go to them when they need him."

"Still. I don't want you to think I used you. That this was just a fling."

Mia's eyes burned with tears she refused to cry. "I don't think that." She kissed him again. "Maybe next Christmas?" She grinned, hoping to calm herself and to ease his guilt.

"I'll call you."

"Please do." She smoothed her fingers over his face. "I'd like to know that the kids are okay."

Savi gave her a slow nod. He cupped the back of her neck and held her still for a long kiss.

"You're an incredible woman, Mia."

With that, he reached for the smoothie and turned his back to her. Mia stayed rooted to her spot by the counter and watched him cross back through the room to his luggage. She opened her mouth to offer help, but he tucked the smoothie between his arm and his side, grabbed the handle of his suitcase, and headed to the main door.

A knot of emotion blocked her throat when he left without a backward glance. Once the door closed behind him, she let the tears go. Not a lot. There was no sobbing, no hysteria, just a few sad tears.

She had said it. She had let it slip when she said *the man I'm falling for.*

And Savi had simply said she was an incredible woman.

Odds were, the past few days, all the things they had said to each other, were said in the thrill, the heat of the moment. Caught up in how good they felt together.

Which mean that most likely, Mia might never hear from him again. Unless he did call her to let her know how Aszia was.

And if he didn't, she might call him just to ask. Because it mattered.

To keep busy, she went to work on the casita. Mia knew Toni had someone who cleaned the house and the casita, but it was good to stay busy. She pulled the sheets from the bed she had shared with Savi and threw them in the washer. Tidied the bedroom and living area.

When she had first arrived here, she had been totally okay with hanging out alone for a few days. Maybe meeting some friends for drinks or dinner. And then going back home to have a late holiday with her family. Now, two days before Christmas, after spending the last few days with Savi, she was lonely. If she wasn't moping over Savi being gone, she was missing her brother and sister. Her parents. She could call them. But she was afraid to. They would hear something in her voice, something would give her away, that she was upset. The last thing she wanted to do—other than spending the next few days alone—was to make her family feel bad for her.

She finished reading the thriller she stared earlier in the week. And she lounged outside for a long time, though this time, she was wearing Savi's shirt with leggings. It was beautiful out, and now, since Savi was gone, even that felt all wrong for Christmas, and she ended up grumpier than she had been earlier.

When her phone rang, she answered it quickly, hoping for news about Aszia. Hopefully, Drew had been mistaken about the severity of her break. And if he hadn't been, hopefully Aszia was in surgery now and would make a full recovery.

Savi's picture on her screen was a knife in her throat. She didn't want to be someone he'd hooked up with on a holiday vacation. She wanted so much more with him.

Mia skimmed her thumb over his smile on the screen before tapping accept.

"Hey."

"Mia."

"Yes. How's Aszia? What's going on? Did you get your flight changed?"

"Can you let me in?"

Mia looked around the patio where she was sitting. The pool water was still and shiny like glass. There was no sound right now, except her conversation with Savi.

"What?"

"I forgot the code. To the door. Can you come and let me in?"

"You're back? What's—why? What's going on?"

"I talked to Blair. And I talked to Aszia. Let me in and I'll tell you."

"You're here?" She laughed softly. "Really?"

She climbed from the lounge chair, knocked her book to the ground, but left it there in her rush to get to the sliding door. She hurried inside, left the slider open behind her, and ran to the front door. The same one Savi had walked out of alone just a couple of hours before.

"Savi!" She threw the door open and squealed when she saw him. Luggage on the porch, he opened his arms and caught her when she jumped into them.

"It feels like I haven't seen you in six weeks." He buried his nose in her hair and breathed deeply. "You feel so good."

"What's going on?" she whispered.

"Sorry I'm back?"

"Shocked, but no. Not sorry." She laughed, arms wrapped tightly around his shoulders. "What happened?"

"Blair finally called. They had Aszia in surgery earlier."

"So, she did break her leg?"

"Compound fracture." He nodded. "Blair had no idea Drew took her phone to call me. I guess he was scared. And he was worried because Blair and Micah talked about postponing the ceremony this afternoon, and Aszia was hurting, so she was crying when they took her in the ambulance."

"But she's okay?"

"She will be." Savi kissed the tip of her nose.

"And you talked to Aszia?"

"I did. And I told her I was at the airport, which was insane, by the way. Told her I was trying to work some magic so I could get to New York to be with her."

"And what?" Mia shook her head. "You're here."

"She said she was okay. I guess the wedding was going

to be very small anyway, so Blair and Micah are going to exchange vows in the hospital chapel. Blair's parents will be there. Micah's brother. The kids."

"And Aszia didn't want you there?"

"She said she would love to see me, but that she doubted I wanted to watch Blair get married. And she asked about you—"

"About me?"

"Yeah, I may have mentioned you the other day. Short story long. She assured me she's okay. And that she'll be happy to see me next weekend."

Mia breathed a sigh of relief.

"What about Drew?"

"Blair put him on the phone, after I asked her to not go postal on him for calling me. He was scared. He and I talked, and he was much more himself. He said he would like to see me, but he said probably I'd rather be with you than at Blair's wedding, and he would see me next weekend."

Mia cupped her fingers around the back of Savi's neck and kissed him.

"So, if you don't have to be there, and you won't see them until next weekend, does that mean you didn't change your flight?"

"I had something finally come up that I could have. I'd have been stuck at the airport for hours, but Blair called. So...I didn't change my flight."

"And so you can be here for Christmas?"

"I can. If you want me here."

Mia smiled. She pressed her thumb to his lips.

"I didn't forget the code," he told her.

"No?"

"No, but after barging in the first time and finding you…topless…and then dragging you to my bed and ravaging you daily and nightly, I thought I'd be a gentleman and make sure you wanted to open the door to me this time."

Mia nibbled on her lip for a moment.

"So, you could still roast a turkey breast for Christmas?"

"I could." He nodded.

"And what about that other thing?"

"What other thing?" Savi tipped his head. Mia's eyes were drawn to the smirk on his face.

"Making love to me by the tree."

"I would love to do that," he told her. "In fact, I don't see any reason that we need to wait."

"No?" She let her gaze roam over his face, thrilled at the playful look on his face.

"We could probably do it right now."

"And if we did, would you still do that to me on Christmas?"

"Yes."

"Savi?"

"Hmm?"

"I'm so happy you came back."

They laughed and kissed again, still wrapped around each other on the porch with his luggage at his feet.

"Savi?"

"Hmm?"

"Where're the cups?"

"In the SUV," he answered. "I was a bit more concerned about getting to you before you found someone to replace me for that Christmas celebration than I was about returning Lane and Toni's cups."

Mia pressed her face to his. "I don't wanna spend Christmas with anyone but you."

"Me, too." He kissed her cheek. "Mia?"

"Hmm?"

"Earlier…" He cleared his throat. "You said something."

"About next Christmas?"

"Not that."

"I told you to call me. About Aszia."

He smiled and shook his head. "You said you were falling for the man who needed to be with his kids."

"I did?"

"You did."

Mia nodded.

"I'm falling, too."

His lips touched hers, tentative and cautious this time.

"Savi, come back inside." She stepped back from him and took his hand in hers. "We have to celebrate Christmas. Starting now."

Savi grabbed his suitcase and followed Mia into the house. The big Christmas wreath on the door banged when he pushed the door closed.

"About next Christmas." He let go of the suitcase and scooped her up in his arms. "Let's just plan it now. To be safe."

"Good idea."

He moved to carry her toward the casita, but she shook her head.

"I put the sheets in the washer."

"So." Savi eyed the tree. "We really are going to do this by the tree."

"Savi?"

"Hmm?"

"Are you sure? You're okay here? Because I get it if you want to be with your kids."

"I'm okay here," he promised her. "I know my kids. They're okay. I'm right where I need to be."

"What did you tell them? The other day? When you told them about me?"

"Just that they didn't need to worry about me spending Christmas alone, because I was with you."

"I don't have a present for you to open," she whispered.

Savi dragged his gaze down over her lips and her shoulders and breasts, still loose under his T-shirt.

"The hell you don't, Mia."

Chapter 1

Ava

When you take your wedding ring off after wearing it for nineteen years, you're making a statement. It's interesting to see the way people react. Some do a double take, like they have to be sure they saw a bare ring finger when you were talking about the new program you're working on, and you were gesturing wildly because taking your ring off wasn't natural for you and you forgot you did it, and so you don't think anything about it or try to hide it. Some try to be sly about it. They double take. They sneak a peek at your hands again when you stop talking and you're reaching for your wine glass, and some turn to look at a colleague, and they try to be sly about this, too, but you see the curve of their eyebrow, and you know they're thinking *did you know? What's that about? Have you seen Logan? Is he wearing his ring?*

He's not. Logan took his ring off first, and I didn't

even notice until we were packing for this trip to Dallas. We're in the same industry, so we travel together often. Used to be fun, but honestly, it got old after ten or twelve years. Take a fun, whirlwind romance and throw in bills and money and kids and all the drama kids can add to life, and let's not forget exhaustion, and those trips stop being a luxurious get away and become one more thing on the calendar. Kind of like making love. Should be fun, adventurous, special. Instead, it gets stale, and you resent the time you give to your partner because you just want a little *me* time.

Then again, it's not like that for guys, is it? Sex is *me time* for men, especially when they can roll over and go to sleep when it's over.

Logan was folding his button-down shirts to pack in his suitcase. He's a stylish guy—always has been—and I stopped what I was doing to watch him. The shirt he was holding was new, gray and white checked. I looked from the shirt to what appeared to be a new gray sport coat tossed over the end of the bed. Logan continued to pack, oblivious to my interest. I had my hair dryer in hand; I had planned to ask him to stick it in his bag as mine was jammed full.

"Mia's counselor—" I stopped midsentence. I remember that. Watching him as he packed his stuff meticulously. Thinking that he had a better wardrobe than I did. He keeps his fingernails cut blunt and clean. His hands are big and strong. And for nineteen years, he's worn a white gold wedding band on his ring finger.

"What about Mia's counselor?" he asked without looking up at me.

My heart hurt.

Not figuratively. Not like flowery-poetic-love-story-heart hurt. It hurt like when your ob-gyn presses and squeezes your ovaries during a pelvic exam. Pain that's sharp and severe and then when he releases you, you feel a little crampy and uncomfortable.

When I still couldn't speak, Logan piled the gray and white shirt on a pale blue shirt—folded just as perfectly—in his suitcase and looked up at me. He wears glasses sometimes instead of contacts, and recently, he switched from the wire-rimmed rectangle lenses he's worn for years to fashion frames.

My husband of nineteen years was dressing like a twenty-year-old guy and not wearing his wedding ring.

Yes, before you ask, I'll just tell you. We're going through some things. At twenty-five, when we got married, I was naïve enough to believe we were different. We were wildly in love and crazy about each other, so there wouldn't be any bad times. Nineteen years later, I know better. Show me a marriage without strife, without growing pains and blow ups, and I'll call bullshit.

We talked about separation one night before we were packing for Dallas, but *we* hadn't made any decisions. Apparently, Logan did. Without telling me. Symptomatic of our marriage, I guess.

"Logan." I dropped the hair dryer on the bed and propped my hands on my hips.

"What?" He straightened, the scowl on his face almost more familiar to me now than his smile. "What'd she do—"

Mia, our seventeen-year-old daughter, has a long history of getting into trouble, so I could almost forgive his scowl. But I felt like his fingers—including his bare ring finger—were squeezing my neck and cutting off my air.

"Really?" I whispered. A flash of guilt eased his scowl to a slight frown, but Logan avoided my eyes. "Now?"

"We talked about this, Ava."

There was no anger in his words. Just regret. Defeat. I think that's what scared me most. If Logan was done with anger, done with shouting matches, we had already moved on through the second stage of marriage. I remember fear of losing him, of losing our life together, chasing a chill up my spine, over my skin.

He swung his gaze to me, his blue eyes pinning me in place. They used to turn me on; now they were cool and indifferent, and if there's anything worse than anger or even hatred, it's indifference.

"But we didn't—. Logan, we didn't decide…"

He hissed a sigh and propped his hands on his hips. The aggression in his stance made me move. I felt like a stranger, an unwelcome, *unwanted* stranger rather than his wife. Hunching my shoulders, I folded my arms over my chest to protect myself.

"I think it's for the best," he mumbled.

The best for whom?

I didn't ask. Truth? It might be. For a few days. For a short time. Mia and Jake used to moan and groan over our public displays of affection. Logan used to be the husband who couldn't walk by me without patting my ass or copping a feel. We used to hug a lot. Snuggle on the couch for evening TV. Close and lock the bedroom door even if the kids were up and running around.

These days we're either at each other's throats over bills or the kids or the dog, or we go days without acknowledging each other. Sure, Mia's behavior puts a lot of strain on our marriage, but I'm sure our issues are beginning to bleed into her behavior. Detention's become a regular thing for her, and I doubt Logan and I fighting all the time is good for Jake. No, marital problems don't cause learning disabilities, but I'm sure the stress, the tension in the house, makes our son feel anything but safe.

Breathing room could be dangerous, though. Which is why I didn't give in before when we talked about a trial separation. While the thought of not feeling judged on every move I made was appealing, making it real—living apart for just a week, even—felt like giving up. The beginning of the end.

Logan has a thing for Charlotte Benz. I've heard the whispers. Always a flurry of them whenever Logan and Charlotte are in the same room together. Funny, there's something about a whisper that's so much louder than casually spoken words. Maybe because they imply something bad, something that should be hidden. People tend to rubber neck a whisper just the same as they do fatal traffic accidents.

Logan's decision to take his ring off before we left for Dallas felt fatal.

Even if I wouldn't have heard the whispers, I knew. Did our colleagues, our friends, really believe I could sleep beside my husband every night and not know he was attracted to someone else?

We finished packing in the uncomfortable kind of quiet that makes you feel like you're bumping up against each other's space and the accidental touches are unwelcome, so you hurry to get done and end up more reckless, and it just keeps happening. Logan slept in the spare room. That alone might not have been so bad, but the way he said goodnight was painful and awkward.

He spoke to my reflection in the mirror in our bathroom. In his athletic shorts and the T-shirt that showed not only his hard shoulders and wide chest, but also the beginning of a spare tire around his middle, he met my gaze for a few seconds. I paused in the act of washing my face—the skin around my eyes itchy from the tears I hadn't been able to stop earlier when we were packing.

He started to say something, but he drew up short and just stopped and pressed his lips together. My throat too tight to talk, I waited. Logan hung his head for a second, and I had the ridiculous thought that maybe he had changed his mind and was going to say so. That rather than living apart and letting the problems in our marriage grow bigger to fill the space between us, we should work on them together and let our love fill in that space.

But he only huffed a quick breath and looked up at me again and shrugged. The way his voice broke when he said goodnight—just *goodnight,* not *goodnight, Ava,* not *I love you*—didn't mean much, because the shrug killed me. Another vicious squeeze on my heart.

I knew Charlotte Benz would be in Dallas. She got married a few years ago, and for a while, I was naïve enough to believe that made everything okay. I had watched them flirt, and I laughed it off with the rest of the gang, because I believed that Logan loved me.

I went to bed that night wondering if Logan loved me *enough.*

ABOUT THE AUTHOR

TE Sheridan loves to read—anything—loves to write—again, she would rather not be nailed down to one particular genre—and loves to travel. She and her happily-ever-after love live in the Midwest, have two children, and live & love life to the fullest.

Writing under her other name—the one that recently decided to experiment with some new, grittier ideas and a pen name—TE is the author of thirty women's fiction and contemporary romance novels and recently decided to experiment with a pen name. As TE Sheridan, she is the author of the Wild Canyon Estates Stories. Lipstick & Liars is her first stand-alone contemporary romance novella.

You can visit TE online at www.tesheridan.com

ALSO BY TE SHERIDAN

Goodnight Kisses, Wild Canyon Estates Stories, #1

Kiss & Make Up, Wild Canyon Estates Stories, #2

Sealed With a Kiss, Wild Canyon Estates Stories, #3

One Kiss, Wild Canyon Estates Stories, #4

Blow Me a Kiss, Wild Canyon Estates Stories, #5

Lipstick & Liars